HO YI THE ARCHER
and Other Classic Chinese Tales

HO YI
THE ARCHER
and Other
Classic Chinese Tales

Retold by
SHELLEY FU

Illustrated by
JOSEPH F. ABBORENO

Chinese Calligraphy by
DR. SHERWIN FU

LINNET BOOKS
North Haven, Connecticut

First published 2001 as a Linnet Book,
an imprint of The Shoe String Press, Inc.,
2 Linsley Street, North Haven, Connecticut 06473.
www.shoestringpress.com

Library of Congress Cataloging-in-Publication Data

Fu, Shelley, 1966-
   Ho Yi the archer and other classic Chinese tales / retold by Shelley Fu ; illustrated by
Joseph F. Abboreno ; Chinese calligraphy by Sherwin Fu.
      p. cm.
   Includes bibliographical references.
   Contents: Pan Gu and the creation—Nu Wo, the mother of mankind—Ho Yi the
archer—Journey to the West—Man in the Moon—Story of the white snake—
Heavenly river.
   ISBN 0-208-02487-5 (lib. bdg. : alk. paper)
   1. Tales—China. [1. Folklore—China] I. Abboreno, Joseph F., ill. II. Fu, Sherwin. III.
Title.
PZ8.1.F97 Ho 2001
398.2'0951—dc21

00-069436

The paper in this publication meets the
minimum requirements of American National
Standard for Information Sciences–Permanence
of Paper for Printed Library Materials, ANSI Z39.48—1984. ∞

Design by
Carol Sawyer of Rose Design

Printed in the United States of America

In memory of my grandmother, Maria Cheng,
who was patient, gentle, strong, and loving.

Contents

Acknowledgments

Thanks to my parents, without whom this book would not have been possible. They taught me Chinese and never let me forget my roots. Thank you, Mother, for telling me these stories when I was a little girl. Thank you, Father, for helping me with this book by sharing your immense knowledge.

I also thank Gary Sampson for all his help, encouragement, and most all, his kind friendship. I miss you, my little Mozart. And of course, thanks to Diantha Thorpe, who has my deepest gratitude for giving me the opportunity to publish my first book. Last but not least, thanks to Dr. Raouf Mama, whose advice and support were a great help.

Preface

✻

The stories in this book were derived from many sources. The written texts that have survived are often very sketchy and sometimes present different interpretations and plots. To fill in gaps in the written versions and resolve discrepancies, I have used discretion in adding to or simplifying and interpreting these tales in order to make them as interesting as possible. In the same spirit, I have made minor modifications to the tales to make them consistent with each other. These modifications include the addition of dialogue, and, in some cases, episodes and references to characters that are introduced in other stories.

This book includes an introduction that discusses Chinese history, politics, and religion and how these forces affected classic Chinese stories. The introduction also provides background that will help the reader better understand the stories presented. It is followed by the three parts of this book: tales of creation, morality tales, and tales of love. The creation tales present ancient Chinese beliefs regarding the origins and characteristics of the world. These stories also introduce Chinese religious and ethical beliefs. The morality tales further explore the Chinese religious and ethical ideology. The love tales encompass many of the themes introduced in the first two parts. Each story is followed by a proverb from Chinese literature appropriate to its theme and also by notes that explain and interpret the story. Also included are a pronunciation guide, a list of characters, and a further reading and multimedia resources guide.

I have tried to present the stories in this book as I remembered them from my childhood and to preserve the essence of the tales. This collection includes some of the most beloved and famous of the Chinese stories. They are as well known to the Chinese as, for example, the most famous Grimm fairy tales are to Westerners. This book is not meant to be an academic exploration of Chinese literature and classic Chinese tales, but rather it is written to entertain and enlighten the reader.

Introduction

The origins of Chinese folktales include history, songs, theater, and the oral tradition of storytelling. Undoubtedly, storytelling was the earliest way these stories were handed down from generation to generation. They were sometimes translated into songs and vice versa. By about 1100 BC, many stories we now think of as folktales were common in "historical" accounts. These stories explained the origins of natural phenomena and document-ed the lives and deeds of semi-legendary figures and were believed to be true. They were written in a very factual style in order to record what was thought of as scientific or historical information and often consisted only of outlines.

During the Han Dynasty (206 BC to AD 220), literature flour-ished as the great masters of the era used the refined language of the court to record popular folktales and songs. During this peri-od, most Chinese literary works were written in *wen yen wen,* or the classical Chinese language. The combination of refined lan-guage with lively folk elements resulted in some of the finest early examples of Chinese literature. However, by the beginning of the T'ang Dynasty (AD 618 to 907), the early creativeness of the Han Dynasty degenerated into a highly stylized and excessively ornate type of literature.

It was during the T'ang Dynasty that the first real fiction appeared, with short stories that had riveting plots and highly developed characters. These stories dealt with virtue, social satire, religion, and love and influenced later drama and fiction. Super-stitions documented in the earlier "historical" accounts were thus elevated into the realm of imaginative literature. The stories were written in the elegant *wen yen wen.*

By the Sung Dynasty (AD 960 to 1279), some writers, feeling constrained by the formality of *wen yen wen*, rewrote the earlier historical accounts and recorded folktales using the common language of China, called *bai hua*. These stories were very popular but were not respected as "real" literature. However, they are often much more colorful and poetic than the writings of the respected classical writers.

It was also during the Sung Dynasty that the tradition of storytelling underwent a glorious renaissance. This rebirth was the result of the rising importance of a new middle class in China. Before then, Chinese society consisted of five broad social classes. In decreasing order of importance, these classes consisted of aristocrats, scholars, peasants, artisans, and merchants. All this changed when previously despised merchants and artisans began making a lot of money from trading their goods with other cities and countries.

As a result, teahouses became very popular, especially with merchants and other lower middle-class people seeking entertainment with their newfound leisure and money. These teahouses were delightful resting places after a hard day's work, and they served tea and simple refreshments such as peanuts and other snacks. As more teahouses opened up, competition became fierce. The more successful teahouse owners hired professional storytellers to entertain their guests for free. Because the customers arrived at different times, the storyteller would tell jokes and anecdotes until the teahouse audience was large enough and then begin his tale. His performance often included singing, poetry recital, and acting.

This trend not only spread and proliferated Chinese folktales, it also affected their content. New stories were told that had merchants or other lower middle-class heroes that appealed to the teahouse audiences. No longer were heroes of stories noble figures who had very few shortcomings. They were often ordinary and very human. Many of these stories tell of common men who struggle to win beautiful princesses in marriage and high stations in life.

With the invention of moveable-type printing in China during the Sung Dynasty, more and more of the previously illiterate masses became literate along with the increasingly prosperous merchant and artisan classes. The rise in literacy made *hua ben* popular. These *hua ben* were outlines written in *bai hua* that helped storytellers remember plots. The hua ben told many of the same stories heard by teahouse patrons and eventually inspired the Chinese novel.

Later, in about the fourteenth century, many plays were written based on the earlier orally transmitted stories. Plays had once been the exclusive entertainment of the rich and elite, but during the Sung Dynasty, actors began forming troupes that toured the country and entertained a large cross-section of society. New stories sprang into being from these plays, which were often performed at festivals. Because they were meant to entertain, the stories often contained poetry, song, dance, and highly elaborate plots and characters not found in the earlier brief "historical" accounts.

During the Ming Dynasty (AD 1368 to 1644), in addition to poetry and essays written in *wen yen wen*, which continued the tradition of classical writings, there was literature written in *bai hua*. This type of literature began to thrive and eventually enlivened drama and the novel. Many great works of this period were based on stories made popular during the Sung Dynasty.

Religion also influenced Chinese folktales. The two major Chinese religions were Taoism and Buddhism. Buddhism was introduced to China in AD 67 but did not become popular until the early half of the sixth century, but Taoism was made popular about four centuries earlier. Taoism is named after Lao Tze (603 to 531 BC), a great Chinese philosopher. Taoists believed in the relationship between man and nature. Taoism influenced literature by stressing the freedom of the individual and thus inspired writers to develop their own styles uninhibited by earlier literary conventions. Buddhists also influenced literature by writing moral tales to teach followers the tenets of Buddhism. Some of the earliest tales were based on Buddhist religious sermons. These stories have moral dimensions that promote virtues central to Buddhism, such as patience, moderation, and a respect for life.

Traditional Chinese stories finally came into their own after the establishment of the Communist Party in China in the 1920s. Long regarded as common, these tales weren't looked upon as a true form of literature until the 1930s, despite the fact that the songs and oral renditions of the tales had inspired so many great Chinese writers of the past. The Communist government praised these tales because first, they were written in the simple and beautiful *bai hua* of the common people. Thus, they represented a triumph over the aristocratic minority, who read and wrote *wen yen wen*. Second, because they were written in *bai hua*, they presented an invigorating "new" form of literature that replaced literature written in *wen yen wen*. Traditional Chinese stories consequently became more popular because they were promoted by the Communist Party as symbolic of the power of the people under Communism over the autocratic emperors of old.

Today, traditional Chinese tales offer a glimpse of the richness, beauty, and down-to-earth spirit of Chinese culture. It is my hope that the reader of this book will gain insight into a colorful ancient civilization. Chinese religion, philosophy, and tradition permeate all of the tales, and yet they all deal with human universals such as self-sacrifice, wisdom, gentleness, vanity, greed, ambition, and love. Although many of the Chinese beliefs and traditions recounted here may seem strange to Western readers, these and all classical tales have survived for so long because of their universal appeal. Ultimately, they remind us of our shared humanity.

TALES OF CREATION

創世

Pan Gu and the Creation

The Chinese believe that in the beginning, the universe was empty except for a big ball of energy shaped liked a chicken egg. This ball of energy had existed since the beginning of time and was called Chaos. Inside the egg, only mist swirled about until one day, the first living creature formed in Chaos.

His name was Pan Gu, and he is the ancestor of us all. After he was formed, he slept for a long time while his body grew bigger and bigger. At first, his body was very small. But after 18,000 years, he grew so extremely big that Chaos could no longer hold him. His strong and heavy head poked against one end of Chaos, and his sturdy feet strained against the other end.

By this time, Pan Gu was enormous beyond measure. In the small and narrow space of Chaos, Pan Gu was cramped and uncomfortable. One day, he became so uncomfortable that he awoke. He opened his eyes in amazement. Beyond the haziness of Chaos, Pan Gu saw darkness so inky that nothing else was visible.

"I'll soon change this situation," thought Pan Gu to himself. He stretched out his hand and made an immense fist, which he struck against the wall of Chaos with all his might. *Ka-bam!* The shell of the egg of Chaos cracked.

As the stuff of Chaos leaked out into the darkness, the clear and light energy, called the *Yang* by the Chinese, curled upwards and formed the beautiful blue sky. The heavier, murkier elements, called the *Yin,* sank to form the earth. After Chaos was divided, the universe became a bright wide space. But the distance between sky and earth was very small, and the elements of sky and earth would frequently mix. Pan Gu couldn't stand up straight in this space and felt like dividing the two so that more distance separated them.

Finally one day, Pan Gu was so bothered that he planted his huge feet on the ground and his hands against the sky. Pan Gu grew an inch every day, and the sky was accordingly pushed one inch higher each day and the earth grew one inch thicker from the pressure of his heavy weight. Time passed. Day after day, Pan Gu stood between heaven and earth, not daring to let go of his hold on the sky, afraid that heaven and earth would mix and all would revert to Chaos.

His salty sweat streamed down from his forehead, stinging his eyes, but he couldn't mop it away. It flowed down his body and fell as rain and dew onto the ground, where it collected into pools to form the seas and oceans.

The work of supporting the sky was extremely hard, and Pan Gu could not suppress a deep sigh of suffering. His breath turned into the floating clouds and the wind, and the sound of his sigh became the rumbling thunder. Over many, many years, he saw the heavens slowly rise and the earth grow thicker and thicker, and he rejoiced.

Finally, after another 18,000 years, the sky was very high and the earth very thick. There was no longer any danger of sky and earth mixing. At last, Pan Gu was satisfied and let go his hold. But the strenuous work of holding earth and sky apart for so long had exhausted Pan Gu, and he fell to the ground immediately.

His body became the massive mountains, his blood and body fluids the surging rivers. His sinews and veins transformed into narrow and crooked roads, his skin and muscles the fertile fields. The hairs on his skin turned into the beautiful and multitudinous grass, flowers, trees, and woods. Even his bones and teeth turned into bright, hard gold, brilliant jewels, and precious pearls. His beautiful hair flew up and filled the whole sky with countless bright stars.

Pan Gu was still not dead and observed the changes with great satisfaction. He knew he was dying, but he wanted to gaze upon his work forever. He winked and sent his left eye into the clear sky, where it turned into the golden sun. He winked again, and his right eye also sailed past the clouds and turned into the bright and silvery moon. Thus to this day, Pan Gu looks lovingly down upon his greatest creation, the bountiful and beautiful earth.

天地與我並生
萬物與我為一

"Heaven and earth were born at the same time I was, and the ten thousand things are one with me." —Chuang Tzu (fourth to third century BC), from *Discussion on Making All Things Equal.* Translated by Burton Watson.

Notes on
Pan Gu and the Creation

Pan Gu is similar to the earth goddess Gaia in Greek mythology. The bodies of both these entities literally are the earth. However, unlike Gaia, Pan Gu willingly sacrifices himself to the creation of the world, an idea that has fostered the reverence of the Chinese people for the earth. Pan Gu's tireless devotion and creative power are characteristics much admired by the Chinese and extensively celebrated in other stories.

Chaos is disorder, and the world cannot exist without order. Therefore, creation stories in many cultures often discuss the formation of the earth or universe out of Chaos. The story of Pan Gu also discusses the uniquely Chinese idea of the *Yin* and the *Yang*, or the dark and the light. The Chinese do not believe that dark represents evil and that light represents good. Rather, they believe that dark and light are both essential elements of the universe. In later times, they also believed that human beings contained both the *Yin* and the *Yang*. Females were believed to contain more *Yin* (the fertile earth), and males were mostly composed of *Yang* (light). Thus the earth and all its creatures are created from a balance of the forces of *Yin* and *Yang*.

This story is one of the oldest legends in China. There are many versions, although perhaps the most famous is presented in *A Supplement to the Chronicle of Dynasties* by Liu Shou, who wrote in the eleventh century.

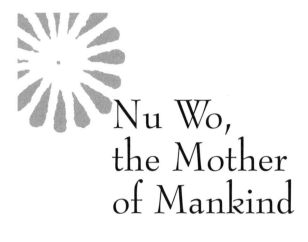

Nu Wo,
the Mother
of Mankind

女
媧
補
天

The Creation of Man

According to ancient Chinese legend, after the world was created, it held only mountains, rivers, grass, flowers, and trees. There were also birds, beasts, insects, and fish, but mankind did not exist. One day, a goddess called Nu Wo looked down on the world from the Celestial Realm, where the gods lived, and decided to visit. She had lived in the Celestial Realm for tens of thousands of years, where she had been very happy at first. After a while, however, her days began to blend one into another seamlessly like a blank, endless roll of rice paper. She needed a change.

The world pleased Nu Wo greatly. She saw beautiful mountains, green waters, birds that flew in the sky, and plentiful beasts

7

roaming the earth. The bright sun and gentle rains caressed the bountiful land, but Nu Wo didn't see a single being that looked like her. She thought about how miraculous the world was and felt that something was missing.

She wandered down to a nearby river to wash her hands. As she knelt down, she saw her reflection in the water. This gave her an idea. The riverbank was made of yellow clay, and she grabbed a handful and began to knead it. As she rolled it into a sphere, she thought to herself, "This clay is so malleable. I can make it into anything I want." Nu Wo began to fashion with the clay a little doll that looked like her. As soon as she set the doll on the ground, it became a living, breathing being. The little girl laughed and ran about playfully. Pulling at Nu Wo's hands, she said, "Mother! Mother!"

When Nu Wo heard the sweet, pretty little girl call her "Mother," she felt her heart fill with love. She caressed the little girl's cheek and asked, "Pretty little child, am I really your mother? What are you called?"

The child answered, "I am called Human Being, Mother."

Nu Wo and the child were inseparable and wandered the world far and wide. Nu Wo taught the little girl the names of all things on earth. She showed the little girl what birds and beasts were, which creatures were friendly, which creatures to run away from, and what was safe to eat. The little girl got into a lot of mischief at first.

One day, she disturbed a hive of bees. The bees swarmed around her. "Mother!" she cried.

"Child, don't be afraid. Stay still and quiet, and they will not harm you. Bees are friends that make honey. If you do not disturb them, they will leave you alone." Nu Wo tried to calm the little girl down.

Just as Nu Wo finished speaking, a rabbit ran out in front of them. It stopped and sniffed the air with its pink nose, looking at them inquisitively with its soft brown eyes. Nu Wo said, "Child, that creature is called Rabbit. It doesn't bite. It is a friend. You can play with it." The little girl and the rabbit cavorted around happily. Nu Wo watched them with satisfaction.

Suddenly, the rabbit ran toward the mountains, and the little girl ran off after it. They ran further and further away until they were no longer visible. Nu Wo was very anxious. "Child! Child! Come back! Please come back!" she cried, but the only answer she got were the echoes of her own desperate cries from the rocky cliffs.

Nu Wo looked for the child for a long time but couldn't find her. Her heart was filled with worry, and her grief weighed upon her like a stone. For many years, Nu Wo wandered about, depressed. Everywhere she looked, she was reminded of her sweet little girl. Finally she gave up searching and wearily sat down on a rock to think.

She thought, "I made one human being out of the yellow clay; I can make another. In fact, I'll make a lot of them. Yes! Then the whole world will be filled with my children. I'll never feel lonely again."

Nu Wo began to make doll after doll out of the yellow clay. She fashioned them to look like the gods of the Celestial Realm. Some were little boys, and some were little girls. As soon as she set them down on the ground, they came to life. They crowded around her, laughing and jumping about. They cried, "Mother! Mother!" Nu Wo had never felt such happiness before.

The Gifts to Mankind

As she did with the first little girl, Nu Wo taught her children. After many years, she had taught them everything she knew. The children learned what things are called and how to make clothing. Nu Wo showed them how to build houses to keep themselves warm and protect themselves from the sun and rain. She also showed them how to grow plants, harvest crops, and tame animals such as sheep and cattle.

As the children grew up, they began to leave their mother and roamed the world until they occupied every corner of the earth. Nu Wo missed each one of them. Instead of returning to the Celestial Realm, she gave up her godhood and stayed on earth as a mortal. She spent all her time wandering from east to west and north to south, visiting her children. Everywhere she went, all people called her Mother, and each human being was her beloved child. Soon, however, she began to notice that something was wrong.

On a beautiful spring day, Nu Wo came to a waterfall where she saw a man sitting on a rock. The man didn't jump up, laugh, or call her Mother. He just sat there by the waterfall. Nu Wo asked him, "Child, what's wrong? Why don't you greet your mother?"

The man answered, "Mother, I was listening to the song of the waterfall. Listen! It is so beautiful!" He fell silent to resume his listening. Nu Wo listened and heard that the song of the waterfall was indeed beautiful. She didn't want to disturb the man and left silently.

A little later on, she wandered into a wood, where she saw a maiden sitting under a tree listening to two nightingales singing. She also didn't jump up and greet Nu Wo. Nu Wo sat down next to her and asked, "Child, are you listening to the song of the nightingales?"

"Yes, Mother! Their song is so lovely. If I could sing like them, I would be so happy." Nu Wo lowered her head, thinking, "Something is missing from their lives!"

Nu Wo walked to a nearby river whose banks were thick with reeds. After much thought, she fashioned a flute from thirteen river reeds. It was the first musical instrument ever made. After calling her children to her, she began to play the flute for them.

They were entranced! Here was music even fairer than the sound of the waterfall, the song of the nightingales, or their gentle mother's voice. Nu Wo taught them how to make flutes of their own, and soon they invented other musical instruments.

Many more years passed, and all seemed well. Everywhere she went, Nu Wo's children greeted her happily as they had in the past. They flourished. Unfortunately, this felicity was not to last. One day, Nu Wo came upon a group of men and women weeping.

"Why are you so sad, my children?"

"Mother! Mother!" they cried. "Something is wrong with Lin! He lay down to sleep, and now we can't wake him. Please come help us!" Nu Wo examined Lin. He was not breathing, and his heart was not beating.

Lin's death was the first in the human realm. Nu Wo was heartbroken because there was nothing she could do. She thought, "What if all my children die? The birds, the beasts, all other creatures, even insects, have children and multiply generation after generation as all other living creatures do. Why shouldn't my children do the same? That way, they'll be here forever."

She paired her children off into couples—one male and one female. Man and woman became husband and wife. Soon, Nu Wo's children were having babies of their own, and the permanence of mankind was assured. In time, Nu Wo was surrounded with grandchildren and great-grandchildren. Now wherever she went, she was called "Mother," "Grandmother," and "Great-grandmother."

The Sky Collapses

Nu Wo and her children were happy, and they had no idea that a great calamity was soon to befall them. One year, the God of Fire and the God of Water met each other on the road. They had been enemies from time immemorial. They glared at each other.

"Get out of my way!" snarled the God of Water.

"YOU get out of MY way, or I'll send you to visit your ancestors!" thundered the God of Fire.

Without another word, they began to fight. The God of Water summoned all the creatures of the waters to help him in the battle. At his call, crab, shrimp, turtle, and lobster generals led countless troops of fish and other creatures to do his bidding in wave after giant wave.

The God of Fire was not to be outdone. He summoned the creatures of fire, awe-inspiring dragons, magnificent phoenixes, and ferocious centipedes. The God of Fire also had a magical golden fan. With one wave of the fan, he kindled tiny flames into gigantic walls of fire.

Although the fire creatures were outnumbered, the God of Fire eventually prevailed, thanks to the wondrous power of the magical fan. The water creatures could not stand the onslaught of his armies. Their moist skins got scorched, and many were boiled alive as the fire evaporated the waves of water. They retreated with great losses.

In tremendous frustration, the God of Water butted his head into one of the pillars that hold up the sky. Because of his stubborn nature, his head was harder than cast iron. The pillar broke, and a large portion of the sky came tumbling down. With it came a torrential flood as waters of the Celestial River came pouring out.

At the same time, the broken pieces of the sky rained down upon the earth as fiery meteorites. The meteorites set the woods everywhere on fire and cracked giant craters in the earth. From under the ground in one of the craters, an immense black dragon emerged and flew into the sky. It began to devour all the people it saw.

Everywhere people were dying. Some died in floods and some in fiery infernos. People also died of starvation as the crops were burned or flooded away, and the dragon devoured most of the others. The survivors all flocked to Nu Wo's side, crying, "Mother! Mother! What are we going to do?"

Nu Wo's grief was extreme when she saw the state that her children were in. She told them to dry their tears and be brave. "In these hard times, we must have the strength and courage to help ourselves," she counseled, and she advised her children to put out the great fires that raged everywhere.

While they were doing this, Nu Wo went to visit the God of Fire. She said to him, "You and the God of Water are both mankind's good friends. When you aren't fighting with each other, all is well for man. However, when you fight, mankind suffers horribly. Just look at all the damage you've caused!" The God of Fire was ashamed of his behavior. Embarrassed, he lowered his head and agreed not to fight with the God of Water anymore.

Nu Wo next visited the God of Water and also berated him. The God of Water was also repentant. "I don't even remember why we were mad at each other in the first place," he admitted with chagrin. "But what can I do? The sky is already broken," he shrugged noncommittally.

Nu Wo saw that neither god would help her repair the damage, but at least they agreed not to battle anymore. She returned to her children. Her first concern was to slay the ferocious black dragon. She armed herself and her children, and together they went to find the dragon. He was dozing at the foot of a mountain after a particularly satisfying day of hunting for humans. Leading the attack, Nu Wo charged at the dragon with her sword.

The dragon saw the angry mob advancing with Nu Wo in the lead, a determined frown on her face. Frightened, it turned tail to run, but it had eaten so many people that it was sluggish and could hardly move. Together, Nu Wo and her children slew the enormous beast. But still the waters from the Celestial River rained down upon the world unceasingly from the hole in the sky. There was no other solution than to mend the hole.

Nu Wo Fixes the Sky

At first, Nu Wo tried to use clay to mend the hole, but it was unreliable when it dried. One little quake, and it would collapse again. Also, its muddy color made unsightly blotches against the beautiful blue background of the sky. Nu Wo tried to use wood logs next, but the water still leaked through the gaps between them. Then she attempted to nail brass plates over the holes. This method was also unstable and leaky, and the plates clanged deafeningly when the wind blew.

"How can I fix the sky so that it is as strong and beautiful as before the catastrophe?" she wondered. She wanted a substance that was strong enough to hold the Celestial River in and yet that matched the clear radiance of the rest of the sky.

Nu Wo thought and thought. Eventually, she decided to melt down five-colored stones and use the liquid ore to mend the sky. These stones were dazzlingly beautiful and sparkled red, yellow, blue, white, and black—the primary colors from which all other colors on earth are derived. They were rarer than the finest diamonds. Some were buried deep under the ground, some were located under the sea, and some were at the tops of high mountains.

Because men and women everywhere were busy trying to put out the raging fires, Nu Wo decided to mine for the precious five-colored stones by herself. She dug deep under the ground. After she had found all of the buried five-colored stones, she dived again and again to the bottom of the sea for them. Soon she had gathered all the five-colored stones that lay underwater. Next, Nu Wo climbed all the tall mountains she could find to search for the stones.

At last, after a thousand hardships and much suffering, Nu Wo found all the five-colored stones in the world. She transported them all to a rocky peninsula near the sea. Soon she had a huge pile. Then, she and her children went to harvest straw. They gathered many thousands of bundles and carried them to a depression in the rock near the pile of stones.

Nu Wo then lit the enormous pile of straw, and she and her children began shoveling the five-colored stones into this fiery furnace. They melted slowly into an opalescent liquid. The heat was so intense that No Wo told her children, "Step back! You'll get burned if you stay too close. I will take care of everything." The children moved away and gathered on the shore nearby. Nu Wo then took a long-handled ladle and began applying the liquid ore to a small hole in the sky. After the liquid cooled, Nu Wo patted the mended spot. It was as sound and as lovely as the rest of the sky.

Nu Wo was overjoyed. "Look!" she cried to her children, "it worked!" The children clapped and shouted and danced. They were saved! Nu Wo began to work in earnest and poured ladle after ladle of the liquid into the holes. The heat made her sweat pour, and she was soon blinded by perspiration and soaked to the skin. The flames seared her skin and her throat became parched. It was unbearable. But Nu Wo looked toward her children, who were still celebrating and singing. She saw them all watching, encouraging her, smiling and waving. She smiled back and bravely kept on working.

Thanks to Nu Wo's hard work, the sky was eventually mended and made as beautiful as always. It was impossible to tell where the holes had been, and the waters of the Celestial River ceased to rain down upon the earth. Nu Wo's entire body was scorched and achy, and she was dead tired. She felt that if she didn't sit down and rest, she would collapse. As she sat on the ground, her children came up to her. They had tears of joy in their eyes and thanked her for her miraculous work.

However, one man didn't thank her or clap and sing with the others. In fact, he had a thoughtful frown on his face.

"Child, what are you thinking about? Why do you look so concerned?" Nu Wo asked.

"Mother, is it true that because a pillar that held up the sky got knocked down, the whole sky collapsed?"

"Yes, that is so."

"Well, I'm worried that with no pillar to hold up the sky as before, all your hard work will have been in vain. What if the dome of heaven collapses again? The original support is gone. Can we trust that the sky is as firmly in place as before?"

Nu Wo realized that the man was right. If she didn't think of a solution to this problem, her children were doomed to suffer the same disaster as before. She saw that she still could not rest. With a deep sigh, she heaved herself up from the ground, saying, "He is right. Farewell, children. My work is still not done. I must leave you now, but I'll be back. When I return, everything will be back to normal. Meanwhile, rebuild your houses. Replant the crops. You must carry on with your lives as before the disaster." She waved to them sadly and walked away.

The Pillars That Hold Up the Sky

Nu Wo's first thought was to use mountains to replace the collapsed pillar, but this solution was not as simple as it first seemed. Exactly how does one go about moving a mountain? Nu Wo wandered thoughtfully toward the sea. Far offshore, a giant turtle spirit was playing in the waves.

The huge turtle was a supernatural being. It possessed great wisdom from having lived so long, and it could read minds. It swam up to Nu Wo and said, "Mother of mankind, don't worry. I will let you chop off my four legs to use as pillars to hold up the dome of heaven." Gentle Nu Wo felt horrible about harming another creature, especially a spirit of the Celestial Realm. She was unwilling to hurt the turtle. When the spirit saw Nu Wo hesitate, it chewed off its own legs.

Nu Wo's kind heart broke to see this mighty being so helpless. She asked it, "Creature, how will you be able to swim without your legs?" So saying, she took her outer robe off and tore it into four pieces. She tucked the pieces into the places where the turtle's legs had been. Now the noble turtle had four flippers instead of four legs. That is why some turtles have legs, and some have only flippers.

When Nu Wo went to place the turtle's legs as four pillars to support the sky, she saw that the two front legs were shorter than the hind legs. This caused the sky to dip down at a slant. From that day on, all the stars, the sun, and the moon rotate in the sky, constantly sliding down towards the earth.

Now the dome of heaven was firmly supported. In fact, you can only see the places where it was mended at sunrise or sunset. They shimmer at these times because of the five-colored stones, and they look even more beautiful than the original sky because of their many colors.

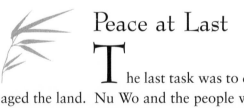

Peace at Last

The last task was to quench the floods that ravaged the land. Nu Wo and the people went to the furnace used to melt the five-colored stones and shoveled the ashes from the furnace into the flood waters to quench them. They started from the northwest and slowly worked their way south, using baskets to carry the ashes.

At first, they used the ashes liberally and reclaimed much of the land. Gradually, they started to run out of ashes, but by that time, they felt that they had done enough and stopped working. That is why the land in the northwestern portion of China is more elevated than the southeastern part. All the flood waters ran toward the southeast and formed the South China Sea.

The sky was now mended, and the earth was reclaimed from the flood. All was as before the great catastrophe. Everywhere, the people rejoiced and held a great celebration that lasted many days. They played their instruments and danced. All of them yelled the traditional Chinese chant, "May Mother live 10,000 years!" When Nu Wo saw how happy they were, her face lit up with a heavenly smile.

In spite of her joy, Nu Wo was exhausted. Her hair, which had been as black and glossy as a crow's wing, was now completely white. Every bone in her body ached. Her hands were blistered and raw from shoveling ashes, and her skin was still scorched from the fires of the furnace of five-colored stones. The pain made it impossible for her to sleep. Her back, so straight and strong when she was a goddess, was now bent, and she had to use a staff to walk. She didn't want her children to see that she was suffering and kept on smiling throughout the festivities.

In the midst of the great celebration and still smiling, Nu Wo closed her eyes forever.

視天下如一家

"Look upon the world as one big family." —Hsu Hsih (AD eleventh century), from *A Memorial to the Throne Written in Hang-chow.* Translated by Shelley Fu.

Notes on
Nu Wo, the Mother of Mankind

Readers may want an explanation of the phrase "May [some-one] live 10,000 years!" To the Chinese, 10,000 represents a very large number. Thus, to wish that someone would live 10,000 years is to wish him or her immortality. It is also interesting to note that the Great Wall of China is called the *Wan Li Tsang Tsin* in Chinese. Literally translated, this means the "10,000-Li Long Wall" (the *li* is an archaic unit of measure).

The goddess Nu Wo not only created mankind, she also gave her children gifts, similar to Prometheus in Greek mythology, who gave mankind fire. In addition, Nu Wo taught people the skills they required to be self-sufficient, such as how to wear clothing, build shelters, farm, and raise livestock. Thus, when the sky collapses, she expects her children to put out the fires themselves as well as help her kill the dragon and spread the ashes after the catastrophe to quench the floods.

Like Pan Gu, Nu Wo shows an abundant spirit of self-sacrifice and devotion to her creation. Her boredom in the Celestial Realm illustrates her creative ambitions, which are fulfilled after she creates humankind, the only creatures capable of appreciating the beautiful earth and interacting with her on her level. After descending to earth, she gives up her immortality, although she still seems to retain supernatural strength. As a mother figure, she literally works herself to death trying to make the earth a safe place for her children to live.

Nu Wo's story explains natural phenomena such as why the sunset is multicolored, why the land in China slopes down to the southeast, and why the sun, moon, and stars rotate in the sky. Because she created the institution of marriage, the ancient Chinese worshipped her as the goddess of marriage.

Nu Wo's origins as a mythological figure are varied. She is sometimes written of as the wife or sister of Fu Shi, a divinity. Other texts say that her lower extremities are those of a snake. Liu An wrote one of the earliest versions of this tale in the second century BC. Another famous account of Nu Wo is Shi Ma Chen's version in *A Formal Record of the Three Emperors* written during the T'ang Dynasty (AD 618 to 907).

Ho Yi
the Archer

后羿射日

Ho Yi and the Nine Suns

In the time of the ruler Yau during China's golden age, nine suns once appeared in the sky at the same time. It was a great catastrophe for mankind, and this is how it happened. The nine suns were all the sons of the Celestial Ruler, and they lived in a place called Hot Water Valley. There, the seawater was as warm as hot soup because that was where the nine sons bathed every day. At that place was also a great tree tens of thousands of feet tall. This tree was the home of the nine brothers.

At the top of the tall tree stood a jade rooster. Each day before dawn, the rooster would crow. When all the roosters on earth heard the jade rooster's cry, they would all crow too. Then one of the brothers would awake, and the day would break. Before the sun rose in the sky, his mother, the Queen of Heaven, would first bathe him in Hot Water Valley. Then, in a chariot drawn by six dragons, the Queen of Heaven would drive him across the sky until they reached a place called Sorrow Spring. The mother would stop the chariot and watch to make sure the sun had safely descended into the Dim Valley. Then she would return to drive her second son across the sky.

Under the Celestial Ruler's decree, all his sons would take turns one by one bathing and driving across the sky. In this way, no more than one son was ever allowed to be with his mother. Things went on this way for billions of years. Every ninth day, each sun would take his bath and ride the chariot with his mother over the same narrow path, performing the same routine. The suns got very bored. It was even worse when it wasn't their turn, for then they slept all day.

One day, all nine agreed to awake at once and run into the sky without even bathing or getting into their mother's chariot. As soon as the jade rooster crowed, they ran riot gleefully, skipping and jumping all at once across the sky. Their mother was quite distressed and called loudly for them to come back, but they pretended not to hear her.

On earth, the temperature started to rise drastically, and all the plants wilted and died. People had no food or water, and many died of starvation or thirst. It was the worst disaster since the sky collapsed in Nu Wo's time. The people decided to go to their leader Yau for help.

Yau was a good ruler. He loved his people as if they were his own sons and daughters. He saw how much his people were suffering, and his heart broke. But it was an act of the gods—what could he do to stop it? All he could do was fervently pray every day to the Celestial Ruler to remedy the problem.

The Celestial Ruler heard Yau's prayers and agreed that something had to be done. Because he was very busy with other affairs, he referred the matter to his wife. Maybe the Queen of Heaven loved her nine sons too much and was happy to see them all at once in all their glory. Maybe she just felt that they needed to have a good time. At any rate, she upbraided them, but not very force-fully. The nine suns therefore paid her no heed and continued to wreak havoc in the sky and upon the earth.

After some time had elapsed, the Celestial Ruler noticed that he was still hearing Yau's prayers. If anything, Yau's prayers were even more urgent, for with the rebellion of the suns, all manner of hideous monsters and beasts were running wild on earth, for they saw that the natural order had been overturned. After looking into the matter, the Celestial Ruler realized that his sons were still run-ning amok. He decided to rely on his friend, the famous archer god Ho Yi, to discipline them.

Once he received the Celestial Ruler's request, Ho Yi brought his beautiful wife, Tsang-O, down from the sky, and they went to meet with Yau. When Yau heard that the Celestial Ruler had sent them, he was very happy. He took Ho Yi everywhere to see the extreme suffering of the people. Ho Yi saw nine suns hanging in the sky at once, and the weather was hot, unbearably hot. The rivers were dry, and nothing grew in the fields. Many people, cat-tle, and horses lay fallen in the streets, dead or near death.

When Ho Yi saw all this, he said to the nine suns, "Even though you are the sons of the Celestial Ruler, you shouldn't be running amok. You are setting a bad example, and chaos is break-ing out everywhere. Can't you see that people are starving and thirsting to death? Why are you doing this?"

The nine suns ignored him, as if to say, "We are the sons of the Celestial Ruler. Who are you, anyway? You can't control us."

Ho Yi grew so angry that his face turned red. The nine suns surely were being unreasonable! Ho Yi debated what to do. He ignored the decree of the Celestial Ruler. He ignored everything in his anger. From his quiver, he withdrew an arrow, fitted it to his bow, and with his right hand slowly drew his bowstring back. He aimed at one sun and released the arrow. Very rapidly, the arrow flew straight into one of the suns. Suddenly, a giant ball of fire fell from the sky. Golden feathers scattered everywhere. When the

people ran to see, they saw a huge golden phoenix on the ground. The phoenix had three legs. This is what the sun had turned into. When the other suns saw what a mighty archer Ho Yi was, they fled in all directions, but it was already too late.

Ho Yi had shot down one sun, but his anger was still not assuaged. He had brought nine arrows in his quiver, and he started to shoot down all nine suns with lightning speed. When the Queen of Heaven saw that her sons were being killed, she began to wail and tear her hair with grief. Strands of her hair fell down from the sky. Each strand was miles long and finer than the thinnest silk thread but as strong as steel. When each strand was coiled up, the entire coil was no larger than the palm of a man's hand.

Yau, who was standing behind Ho Yi, thought, "What will happen if Ho Yi shoots down all the suns? The earth will turn cold and black. How will my people survive?"

He implored the archer god not to shoot down all of the suns, but Ho Yi was too angry to listen to reason or to anybody. Yau had no recourse but to steal one arrow from Ho Yi's quiver, so Ho Yi shot down only eight of the suns, using up all of the arrows he had left.

Only one sun was left in the sky, and the temperature quickly cooled down. Black clouds appeared in the sky. Even though Ho Yi's quiver was empty, the sun did not know that, and he fled into a black cloud, not daring to emerge. The clouds grew thicker and thicker, and rain began to fall. When the people saw that it had begun to rain, they rejoiced. Some yelled, some laughed, some sang, and others started to till the fields. Suddenly, the rain increased. The people hailed the archer god with the traditional Chinese chant, "Long live Ho Yi! May he live 10,000 years!" You could hear their cries everywhere. Ho Yi was their hero. As a reward, Yau gave Ho Yi a strand of hair from the Celestial Ruler's wife and a golden feather from one of the phoenixes that had fallen from the sky.

But the people could not rest. Poisonous snakes and dreadful beasts still roamed the earth. In the sky flew man-eating birds. Yau begged Ho Yi to eliminate all these fearsome creatures. Altogether, Ho Yi slew many different kinds of monsters of very strange appearance. One looked like a giant ox, with a red body, a human face, and the legs of a horse. With a cry that resembled the wail of a human baby, it would lure its next meal. Ho Yi slew another monster that had the body of a man but the head of a beast. Its teeth were especially long. The ancient books say they were 5 or 6 feet long. Despite the fierceness of these creatures, they were no match for Ho Yi's prowess in archery, and he eliminated them all.

The Celestial Ruler's Decision

Ho Yi thought that his work in the human realm was done. He thought he would return to the sky with his wife and resume his life as a celestial spirit. He said to himself, "I have done so many good deeds on earth, the Celestial Ruler should be very pleased with me. I killed eight of his sons, but it wasn't my fault. It was theirs for not heeding me. In all fairness, surely the Celestial Ruler will understand."

Ho Yi was wrong. The Celestial Ruler was very angry with Ho Yi and immediately banished him and his wife Tsang-O to the human realm. They could not return to the sky.

"But it isn't fair!" cried Ho Yi. "I did no wrong, why can't we return?" Behind him, Tsang-O was crying, and Ho Yi suffered greatly. "I have done her harm!" he said to himself. He and Tsang-O were now mere mortals.

Ho Yi's wife Tsang-O, though beautiful, was a very stubborn woman. When she made up her mind to do something, she would heed no advice or reason. Nonetheless, Ho Yi loved her to distraction. In heaven, they had a very happy marriage, but after being banished to the human realm, Ho Yi was very busy and had no time to spend with Tsang-O. She was very lonely.

She told her husband, "The human realm is unbearably dull compared to the realm of the Celestial Ruler."

"Don't worry, Tsang-O. Wait until I finish my business on earth, then we will try to return to the sky," he would reply to her complaints.

Day after day passed, and Ho Yi's business seemed interminable. As soon as he had finished one thing, a new matter would arise. He really didn't mind the work. Every time he heard the people cry, "Long live Ho Yi! May he live 10,000 years!" he felt a deep fulfillment. In the Celestial Realm, he had never been so celebrated.

"Why are you still working? Tell me truly, when can we go back?" Tsang-O asked her husband almost every day.

"I'm almost done. Don't worry. See how full of suffering these human lives are? How can we leave them this way?" he would reply.

Finally, Ho Yi finished his earthly business. Everything was restored to normal after the recent catastrophic events. Ho Yi was very satisfied with his work. Tsang-O thought that now they could return immediately to the Celestial Realm, and she was happy.

But the Celestial Ruler still refused to let them return. At first, both Ho Yi and Tsang-O suffered greatly. Ho Yi felt that the Celestial Ruler was being unfair. After a time, however, Ho Yi began to feel that life in the human realm wasn't so bad. He wanted to stay, for he was a big hero. Yau showered him with favors and presents and made him a high-ranking nobleman.

"Because there is no justice in the Celestial Realm, why don't we just stay here?" he would say.

Tsang-O saw things very differently. She couldn't agree with her husband. She blamed Ho Yi for everything. "I don't understand. Why did you have to kill them?" she would reproachfully ask about the eight suns.

"It wasn't my fault! You saw them, they were running wild!"

"But they were the Celestial Ruler's sons!"

"Even so, they should not have been allowed to do whatever they pleased. Didn't you see how much mankind was suffering?"

"Mankind! That's all you ever talk about! How can helping mankind enable us to return to the Celestial Realm?" Tsang-O was angry.

"So what if we can't return? We're not bad off at all here," was Ho Yi's reply.

The more they talked, the angrier they became with each other. In the end, Ho Yi would storm out of the house. Every day, Tsang-O would stay at home and cry or sulk. Ho Yi couldn't stand it. Life between the two became unbearable. Every morning, Ho Yi would leave the house and wander he knew not where. Sometimes he stayed away for days.

The Fairy of Lo River

One day during his wanderings, Ho Yi accidentally ran into the beautiful goddess of the Lo River, Fu Fei. It was a beautiful autumn morning, and Ho Yi got into his carriage as usual. Deeply preoccupied, he drove and drove until he had reached the Lo River. He suddenly realized that he had traveled very far from home.

"I probably won't make it home today. Oh well, so what?" Ho Yi asked himself angrily as he thought of the crabby Tsang-O.

All of a sudden, he heard the sound of voices. Going to investigate, he saw a group of beautiful fairies playing by the river. Some were running on the grass, some were singing with the birds, and some were busy in the river playing with the fish. They were all laughing or singing happily. But one fairy all in white with long black hair was sitting by herself on a rock. She wasn't singing or laughing and seemed very lonely.

Ho Yi felt compassion for the lonely maid and slowly approached her. The closer he came, the more clearly he saw her. She was as beautiful as a silver cloud in the sky, as beautiful as a white lotus flower in the river. To Ho Yi, she far outshone all the others in beauty, for her features were far more refined. This beautiful woman was Fu Fei.

Ho Yi was enchanted. For a moment, he felt a pang of guilt. But then he thought about the many bitter arguments he had recently with Tsang-O and saw her features distorted with anger and grief. He quickly put her out of his mind.

When the fairies saw Ho Yi, they shrieked, causing Fu Fei to slowly raise her head. She was not at all surprised, but instead acted as if she were seeing an old friend. She smiled warmly at Ho Yi, even though he had never seen her before. The other fairies calmed down as Ho Yi smiled back and came forward to take her hand. It seemed as if everything in the universe had come to a halt, and a great silence fell. There were only Ho Yi and Fu Fei, and feelings of love flowed between them.

Fu Fei was the wife of the god Old Man River. Old Man River controlled all the rivers of the world and all the creatures within the waters of the rivers. With such a beauty for a wife, Old Man River should have been satisfied. But he wasn't and would carouse everywhere with other women.

Every time Old Man River wanted a new woman, he would set foot on land, bringing with him great floods. He particularly liked to alight on the shores of the Yellow River. Each year, the river flooded, causing great harm to the crops and cattle. That is why every year, the people would throw a fair maiden into the Yellow River to be Old Man River's concubine. They hoped this would keep Old Man River from setting foot on shore. This barbaric practice continued for 2,000 years before it was stopped.

Even though Old Man River loved to dally with other women, he would not allow Fu Fei to see other men. When he heard that Fu Fei and Ho Yi were together, he was furious. He changed himself into a fearsome white dragon and left the river, seeking Ho Yi. From the heavens fell great rains, and thunder crashed deafeningly.

As Old Man River rose into the sky, he saw Ho Yi standing on a mountain, bow in hand, unmoving. When Ho Yi spied the white dragon, he slowly fitted an arrow to his bowstring. Behind him stood the beautiful Fu Fei. Ho Yi proudly stood there, a former god and hero of the people. Old Man River hesitated, for he was a bit afraid. But he couldn't let his wife know he was a coward, so he flew toward them.

Ho Yi released his arrow so swiftly and mightily that Old Man River, though he turned at the last minute, was shot in the left eye. Old Man River fell heavily to the earth, and Ho Yi fitted another arrow into his bow. At that moment, he heard a woman's voice behind him. It was Fu Fei pleading, "Please don't kill my husband!"

Fu Fei pushed past Ho Yi and quickly ran toward her fallen husband. It all happened so fast that Ho Yi was paralyzed. Stunned, he let the second arrow drop. It wasn't him that Fu Fei loved! Ho Yi turned and slowly walked away.

The Journey to Kun Lun Mountain and Tsang-O's Decision

In times of trouble, a person's thoughts turn to home. After his unhappy experience with Fu Fei, Ho Yi again thought of the lovely Tsang-O. "Even though she is stubborn, she is after all my wife. We have had some very happy times together."

He returned to Tsang-O. Time changes many things, and matters between husband and wife greatly improved. But their original problem was still unsolved. How could they regain their status as gods? When they were gods, they had heard of the Spirit of the West, who lived on Kun Lun Mountain and made an elixir of immortality; already being gods, however, they paid no attention to this information. Now they remembered.

Kun Lun Mountain was in the west, very far away. In a cave in the mountain lived a spirit called the Spirit of the West. The ancient books say that the spirit was a friendly soul that would sometimes disguise itself as an amiable old lady. Its true appearance was quite fearsome. Its hair was long and messy. Its fangs were like a tiger's, and it had a tail. Whether it was male or female, no one could tell. This spirit controlled all the evil spirits of the world.

With the Spirit of the West lived three enormous birds with black bodies and red heads who could fly thousands of miles with one wing beat. When these birds saw a beast on earth, no matter how big the beast, they would kill it and bring it back to the Spirit of the West to eat. When the spirit was well fed and happy, it would emerge from the cave and howl, causing all the beasts who heard it to flee in all directions.

According to the legends, on Kun Lun Mountain was a tree that bore fruit. Anyone who ate the fruit would never die. It was from the fruit of this tree that the Spirit of the West made an elixir of immortality. Whoever took the elixir would live forever and never grow old. But the tree rarely bore fruit. It only flowered once every 3,000 years, and even then, the flowers would bear only a few fruits, a process that took another 3,000 years. Yet another 3,000 years were required for the fruits to mature. The precious elixir was therefore very scarce, and the Spirit of the West did not have much of it.

But what mortal doesn't wish to live forever without aging? That is why people flocked to Kun Lun Mountain to seek the Spirit of the West, but very, very few people ever succeeded in meeting it.

First, Kun Lun Mountain was extremely high, and very few could scale it. Second, near the top of the mountain was a very wide, very deep river. Legend has it that anything touching the waters of the river would immediately sink, even a bird's feather, much less a boat. Third, the top of the mountain was surrounded by fire that burned all day and night. Even if one could scale the mountain, cross the river, and pass through the fire, Kun Lun Mountain was huge, and finding the entrance to the Spirit of the West's cave had no guarantee.

"Now that you are no longer a god, can you climb Kun Lun Mountain?" Tsang-O asked Ho Yi doubtfully.

"Why don't I try? It's our only hope," replied Ho Yi without much confidence. Those who wished to undertake the task of seeking the Spirit of the West had to have an iron will, unsurpassed strength, and a little luck, too.

Ho Yi started on the trip, carrying with him his bow and a quiver full of arrows, a bag of provisions his wife had prepared for him, and both their hopes. After many hardships and much time, he succeeded in reaching Kun Lun Mountain. It took much strength to climb the mountain, and the air got thinner and thinner and colder and colder. When he could no longer walk, he crawled. At last he crawled to the river, where he could go no further. He collapsed on the bank and slept on the ground as gratefully as if he were sinking into the best bed in Yau's palace. Ho Yi stayed near the river for three days regaining his strength and trying to think of a way to cross it. Finally, he thought of the coil of hair from the Celestial Ruler's wife that he had kept in his quiver. Despite all the years that had passed, it retained its wondrous strength.

Ho Yi climbed a tree and looked across the river, which was miles wide. On the other side, he saw a similar tree. Tying one end of the hair to his tree and the other to an arrow, he shot the arrow into the tree on the other side. The hair now stretched like a cable miles across the river. Ho Yi grasped it, and hanging from the hair, he began to cross the river hand over hand. Beneath his feet, which were dangling in mid-air, the river roiled and waves leapt up to snatch him, but he was too high up. Just when he thought he could hang on no longer, he reached the other shore.

After a long rest and walking a few miles, Ho Yi reached the wall of fire. Its flames were several thousands of feet high. This time, he immediately thought of the golden feather from the phoenix in his quiver. It is customary in China to worship one's ancestors, and this gave Ho Yi an idea. Quickly, he pulled out the feather, which blazed with golden light, and thrust it before the wall of fire.

"Kneel before this feather, for it is a relic from your ancestor, one of the nine suns," commanded Ho Yi. Because all fire on earth is descended from the fire of the nine suns, the flames had no choice but to kneel until they were only as high as Ho Yi's knees. Ho Yi simply stepped over them.

It took many more days for Ho Yi to find the cave of the Spirit of the West, but at last he stood face to face with it. Even though it chose to appear to Ho Yi as a friendly old lady, Ho Yi recognized the spirit's great power. He respectfully bowed to the spirit and told his story. The old lady commiserated with the plight of Ho Yi and Tsang-O. Pulling out a package of the elixir, she said, "If one person eats the contents of this package, he or she will mount to the sky as a god. If two people share the contents equally, they will live forever and never grow old. It is my last package. Take very good care of it."

Ho Yi thanked the Spirit of the West, very happy in his heart, and immediately began the long journey back through the fire, across the river, down the mountain, and home. Once he was finally home, he told Tsang-O of all that had elapsed.

"Our luck is not bad," he said to Tsang-O. "I got one package of elixir from the Spirit of the West. If we split it, we can live forever. Please put it somewhere safe. We will wait a couple of days, then choose an auspicious day to take the elixir together."

Ho Yi handed the package over to his wife and went off to sleep. After all the grueling hardships he had suffered, he needed to rest both spirit and body.

Ho Yi didn't necessarily want to return to the Celestial Realm. In his opinion, things there weren't that much better than on earth. All he wanted was to live forever with Tsang-O in the human realm, never aging. This was good enough for him.

Tsang-O, however, had other thoughts. Once, she had been a goddess. She felt that she had done no wrong, so why must she be relegated to the human realm for all eternity for something her husband had done? She didn't like it on earth. Human beings were noisy, dirty, pathetic creatures.

"Why shouldn't I just eat all the elixir myself?" she mused. "No, I couldn't do that. He passed through so many hardships to get it. I couldn't be so selfish. But . . . I do want to be a goddess again. I did no wrong . . . ." Tsang-O slowly opened the package.

"I'm sorry, Ho Yi. Please forgive me." So saying, she hurriedly ate the contents.

Tsang-O felt her body grow lighter and lighter until it weighed less than a feather. Her feet left the ground, and she began to float up into the sky faster and faster. After a time, she landed in a very bright place. It was very clean. All the mountains and trees were silver. Everything was silver. In fact, she had flown to the moon!

"It's so beautiful here, so peaceful. This is too good to be true!" Tsang-O sat down to rest. "But where are the other gods? Where are the other people?" Tsang-O began to think that this place was too peaceful. In fact, it was so peaceful it was a little scary. She began to look for other gods and people but could find not a soul. She started to cry, and her sobs echoed off the hard silver mountains and silver trees. They seemed to be laughing at her, mocking her for her selfishness and stupidity.

She began to regret her rash act. Tsang-O thought about what a good life she had had on earth with Ho Yi and wanted to return, but it was impossible. She was stuck on the moon forever. Every night, she would peer toward earth, hoping to see her home, her husband. But the moon is too far away from earth. All she could see was black space and blue oceans.

Ho Yi's Student, Feng Men

The next day, Ho Yi discovered his wife's disappearance. When he figured out what had happened, he was furious. After all his bitter experiences, he hated all the Celestial Realm and all the human realm. Even his own wife had cheated him! Ho Yi began to change. His disappointment in everything was extreme, and he no longer cared if he lived or died.

"There is no justice in the Celestial Realm, and the human realm is filled with deceitful women. Does hell hold anything worse? What's so bad about dying?" he thought to himself. Every day, he went out drinking and carousing. His life had lost all significance.

Ho Yi's temperament grew worse daily. In his home, he beat the servants, and they all fled at the sight of him. But there was one servant named Feng Men whom he didn't beat. Ho Yi was very fond of Feng Men, who was a very capable boy.

"You should learn archery," Ho Yi told Feng Men.

"Please teach me, Master," Feng Men replied respectfully.

"Learning archery is not an easy matter. First, you must train your eyes not to blink. When you are shooting, you must not blink."

Feng Men went home to discipline himself. He would lie on his wife's loom. The loom shuttle would dart back and forth, but he would not blink. At first, it was very hard to get used to, but eventually Feng Men was successful. He returned to Ho Yi.

"Good. You have trained well. Next, you must improve the strength of your eyesight so that you can see very clearly and very far," Ho Yi told Feng Men. Feng Men again returned home, this time for a very long time, to improve his eyesight. He returned to Ho Yi, who told him his eyesight was still not good enough. Feng Men went home again. This time, he tied a small insect to a cow's tail. Every day, he would look at the insect. When he could see it clearly, he would move back a few steps and try to see it clearly again. In time, he could stand very far away and still see the tiny insect on the cow's tail.

"Now you are ready to learn archery," said Ho Yi.

Feng Men was an excellent student, and he learned all that Ho Yi taught him. People said, "Feng Men is a very good archer. Besides Ho Yi, there is not another who can shoot as well as he." When Feng Men heard their words, he was very envious. He thought he was Ho Yi's equal.

One day, Ho Yi and Feng Men went out together. A lot of birds were in the sky migrating from north to south. To test Feng Men's ability, Ho Yi asked his student to shoot three arrows in the sky, one after the other, into the flock of birds. Feng Men obeyed and quickly brought down three birds.

"Not bad at all!" cried Ho Yi happily.

"Master, why don't you try it too?" asked Feng Men.

By then, the birds were dispersing. Some were flying east and some west. Ho Yi raised his own bow, let three arrows fly, and also brought down three birds, but much more rapidly than Feng Men despite the disorder of the flock.

"I'm still not as good as my master," thought Feng Men unhappily. "How can I surpass him?" he asked himself. "Unless he were to die . . . ."

From that day on, Feng Men wished for Ho Yi's death, but Ho Yi was as healthy as an ox. It looked like Ho Yi would live a very, very long life.

"I should just kill him!" thought Feng Men. "But he is my master! How could I kill my own master? If I don't kill him, I'll never be the best archer in the world. I'll never be Number One."

Feng Men finally decided to wait for a suitable opportunity to kill Ho Yi.

One day as Ho Yi was returning home, someone suddenly stepped out from behind a wall and shot an arrow at him. It was Feng Men. Ho Yi, with lightning speed, shot his own arrow back. The two arrows collided in mid-air and fell to the ground. Feng Men shot another arrow. Ho Yi returned fire, and again the arrows collided and fell. In all, Feng Men shot a total of nine arrows, but just as rapidly, Ho Yi returned fire, rendering all the arrows useless. Feng Men then shot a tenth arrow, but Ho Yi had run out of arrows. The arrow hit Ho Yi in the mouth. Ho Yi fell to the ground like a dead man.

Feng Men walked slowly toward Ho Yi, uttering a cold laugh. As soon as he was near, Ho Yi leapt up and spat the arrow out of his mouth. The great archer had caught it in his teeth. This was Ho Yi's best maneuver, and he had not taught it to Feng Men.

Feng Men was terrified. He threw himself on the ground. "Please, please forgive me, Master," he begged. Ho Yi was very angry but did not kill Feng Men. He didn't think it was worth the trouble to kill such a mean-spirited person. Ho Yi felt very betrayed, for he had treated the young man as his own son. He ignored the kneeling, weeping Feng Men and walked away.

This matter made Ho Yi even more bitter, and his disposition worsened even more rapidly. Many of his servants quit, and the servants who stayed were either terrified of him or angry with him.

"We can't go on like this! We should go complain to Yau," some said.

"Are you kidding? Yau loves him and would let him get away with anything. That won't do any good. We should think of another solution," said others.

Feng Men saw that his opportunity had come. He still hated Ho Yi even though his master had spared his life. Strangely enough, he hated Ho Yi even more than before precisely because Ho Yi had refused to kill him.

"Your words are useless," he told the servants. "We should get organized and have a plan. Even though he's a marvelous archer, we are many. What do all of us together have to fear from him? Here's a good plan—tomorrow morning, Ho Yi is bringing us with him to go hunting . . . ."

The next morning was a beautiful autumn morning much like the one on which Ho Yi had met the beautiful Fu Fei. As planned, he took his servants hunting with him. They bagged a lot of game.

"Our luck's good today," thought Ho Yi. That day, his temper was especially good. He had not been so happy for a long time. He thought that everyone was at peace like himself, not dreaming that the outward calmness of his servants hid a fiery rebellion. Suddenly, the weather changed. A black cloud appeared in the sky, growing bigger and bigger. The sun disappeared, and from afar came the sound of thunder.

"Let's go home," said Ho Yi to the servants, but no one moved.

"I said let's go back! Do you hear me?" Ho Yi yelled.

The servants slowly approached. Ho Yi became uneasy and raised his bow.

"Kill him!" someone yelled suddenly.

"Kill him! Kill him!" all the servants began to yell.

Ho Yi fitted an arrow to his bowstring, but before he could shoot, a servant standing behind him raised a big stick and brought it down on Ho Yi's head with all his might. Ho Yi fell off his horse to the ground, not moving.

In the sky, lightning flashed, and thunder roared. It began to rain.

满招损

"Pride invites calamity." —Anonymous, from *The Classic of History,* edited by Confucius (551 to 479 BC). Translated by Shelley Fu.

Notes on
Ho Yi the Archer

Rather than explaining existing natural phenomena, Ho Yi's story is more akin to the best of the Greek myths, which deal with human strengths and weaknesses. The story is set in the time of Yau, an actual emperor who is said to have ruled China during its golden age, sometime around 2300 BC.

The characters in the Ho Yi story are much more developed than the flat and unchanging characters of Pan Gu and Nu Wo in the first two stories of this book. Like the Greek and Roman gods, the Celestial Ruler, his wife, Ho Yi, and Tsang-O all exhibit human characteristics and frailties. Ho Yi himself is a vain character who wants to stay in the human realm because of the adulation of the people. He does not help mankind until the Celestial Ruler orders him to, and he continues to help mankind only because Yau, the ruler of China, treats him with special consideration.

Because Ho Yi killed eight of the celestial sons, he and Tsang-O are severely punished by the Celestial Ruler. Their attitudes represent the anger of mortals at the actions of the gods. In addition, after both Tsang-O and Fu Fei desert Ho Yi, his bitterness at their betrayal poisons his life and the lives of all those close to him. He thus no longer cares about his impending death.

Tsang-O's flaws are obviously pride and selfishness. She feels that the human realm is beneath her and steals the elixir of immortality from her husband in order to rise above her station. Tsang-O's actions oppose the wishes of the Celestial Ruler and therefore represent defiance against the Taoist hierarchy of heaven, which is the celestial government. Taoism is named after Lao Tze (603 to 531 BC), a great Chinese philosopher. Under the Taoist hierarchy, the Celestial Ruler is akin to the Emperor of China. He commands gods such as Ho Yi, Tsang-O, Old Man River, and even the Spirit of the West. The Celestial Ruler has magical powers and, like a mortal emperor, directs troops, which his heavenly generals command. He also enacts the law as the head of a celestial government. Thus, even the gods must obey his word.

Tsang-O's betrayal of Ho Yi also goes directly against the teachings of Confucius (551 to 479 BC), which stress loyalty to the family. Confucius was a philosopher whose writings greatly influenced the Chinese for well over 2,000 years. He is still revered as one of the world's greatest thinkers. Because Confucius also wrote about the duties of the individual to serve the government, Tsang-O's actions are doubly offensive from a Chinese viewpoint. Her punishment is being sent to the moon, a cold, barren, and lonely place in most Chinese tales. In time, some people referred to her as the Goddess of the Moon.

The stories of Ho Yi and Tsang-O are very famous and frequently alluded to in poems of the T'ang Dynasty (AD 618 to 907). The earliest version of the story is in the anonymous *Classic of History,* one of the oldest books in Chinese history, which was edited by Confucius. Another famous telling is presented in *The Commentary of Tzo* written in the fifth century BC by Tzo Ch'iu Ming.

MORALITY
TALES

道德

Journey
to the West

西
遊
記

The Monkey King

There was once a mountain called Flower and Fruit Mountain. On the top of the mountain was a stone egg that had been washed by the wind and rain for thousands of years, becoming inundated with these elemental essences. In time, the egg split open, giving birth to a monkey. As soon as he was born, the stone monkey capered about happily, full of the joy of life. It was not long before the monkey explored the entire mountain. Soon he found a band of real monkeys. Overjoyed at finding his own kind, he told these monkeys about a cave he had discovered behind the curtain of a waterfall.

"Show us! Show us!" they gathered about him, clamoring. "Surely, this cave would be a perfect place to live! We would be safe from tigers and bears. No one would know where we lived."

The stone monkey quickly led them to the cave. All the monkeys were afraid at first of leaping through the waterfall, especially the smaller and younger ones. Undaunted, the brave stone monkey leapt through with one jump. Encouraged, the braver and stronger monkeys followed. When the others saw that they had made it, they all took the leap with much laughing and shouting.

When they had all assembled on the other side of the waterfall, they were exhilarated, for they saw that they were in a clean and spacious cave. After a few hours of exuberant capering, the monkeys suddenly fell silent.

They all gathered around the stone monkey, and the oldest monkey there, a grizzled and wise macaque, bowed respectfully to the stone monkey. "I have been the leader of this band for many years," he said. "But today, you have shown us a safe place to live, all within a few hours of meeting us. Surely in time you will lead us to unparalleled greatness and prosperity. We humbly ask you, stone monkey, to be our king."

Joyfully, the stone monkey replied, "I am honored to accept your leadership. Let me now be known as the Monkey King!" All the monkeys greeted this pronouncement with deafening shouts and hoots of "Long live the Monkey King! May he live 10,000 years!" That night, they had a great feast of the best fruits on the mountain to celebrate their new king and wonderful new place to live, which they dubbed the Water Curtain Cave.

And it was as the old macaque predicted. The Monkey King ruled for many years, and his tribe prospered. From him, they learned all sorts of tricks for stealing good things to eat from men, and they even developed a taste for wine. No one could find the Water Curtain Cave where they lived. Their numbers multiplied, and all the beasts of the mountain soon feared them. Even the mighty tiger was afraid, for when the monkeys banded together, neither man nor beast dared oppose them.

But as the years passed, the Monkey King grew discontented. Although he was still as vigorous as ever and aged much more slowly than the other monkeys, he was afraid of dying. Over the years, he saw many of his tribe die of old age or illness, and he felt a chill whenever he thought of these things. He took his bad temper out on the other monkeys. Because he was a good king, he saw that his ill humor was depressing everybody.

One day, he announced, "Children, I have decided to take a trip. I have recently felt that the God of Death is seeking me out. I need to do some exploring. By taking this trip, I hope to find the secret of immortality."

All the monkeys howled and wept. "Don't worry. I promise to return. In the meantime, I appoint the old macaque as your temporary ruler," the Monkey King said, pointing to that venerable ape, whose fur was now as white as snow. "Heed his word. I expect you all to behave when I am gone," he concluded.

The monkeys all hung their heads and cried. That night, they held another feast to wish their king the best on his travels. But it was not a success, for everyone was subdued and worried.

The Search for Immortality

After the others were asleep, the Monkey King left Water Curtain Cave and Flower and Fruit Mountain. He traveled for many years and learned much. From man, he learned human speech and how to wear clothes. Traveling by sea on a little raft he had built, he reached a land far to the west. There he came upon a beautiful mountain. After walking up the mountain path for quite some time, the Monkey King felt the air turn chilly and thin.

He was just about to turn back when he spied a cave with a little door. Above the door was a sign that said, "Cave of the Slanting Moon and Three Stars." The Monkey King was so taken by this name that he decided to knock. "After all," he reasoned, "this mountain and the name of this cave reeks of magic.

If anyone can teach me how to be immortal, surely it is whoever lives in this cave."

At the sound of his knock, a little boy came out. "Come in," said the child. "My master told me that a stranger seeking enlightenment was going to visit us today. He must have meant you." Delighted, the Monkey King straightened up his clothes and eagerly followed the little boy. In no time, he found himself in front of a distinguished old man.

At one glance, the Monkey King saw that this man was no ordinary mortal. He threw himself at the old man's feet, exclaiming, "Master, please accept me as your pupil. I have come to learn the secrets of immortality from you."

Sternly, the old man said, "Only those pure of spirit and with great patience can learn anything from me. Are you willing to spend many years perfecting yourself?"

"Oh yes, Master," cried the Monkey King earnestly.

In a more kindly tone, the master said, "Well, we shall see. In the meantime, please tell me your name."

The Monkey King was perplexed. "Name? Why, I don't know. I don't suppose I have one. All my life I have been called the Monkey King."

"That simply will not do as a name," replied the master. "You need an appropriate name to study religion. How about Shun Wu Koong? It means 'Aware of the Void.' "

The Monkey King was so happy with his new name that he cavorted about in a most undignified manner.

"Shun Wu Koong!" yelled the astonished old man. "That behavior is unacceptable. If you do not calm down, I will kick you out of my cave this instant!"

Chastised, Shun Wu Koong instantly quieted down. The old man then summoned a boy to show Shun Wu Koong his new quarters. Secretly ecstatic, Shun Wu Koong demurely followed the little boy, convinced that at last he was on the path to immortality.

For many years, Shun Wu Koong spent his time learning subjects that seemed irrelevant to his quest for immortality, such as speech, manners, and calligraphy. In his spare time, he worked at menial tasks such as cooking, weeding the garden, drawing water, and chopping firewood. His cell was small and bare, and the master's disciples had no opportunity for frivolity. However, Shun Wu Koong did not fret. He remembered the old man's first speech to him about patience, and he bided his time.

Finally one day, the master began a lecture about the Great Way, or the Tao as the Chinese call it, to all the disciples. Shun Wu Koong was so happy that he couldn't contain himself and began scratching himself all over in monkey fashion. He had been waiting for this day all along. The old master soon noticed this unbecoming behavior and abruptly stopped talking.

"What are you so happy about, Shun Wu Koong?" he sternly demanded.

"I'm sorry, Master, it's just that your speech has delighted me so much I can't keep still," said Shun Wu Koong contritely, with one final scratch.

"So, you understand the importance of what I'm saying," the old man said and resumed his lecture. Afterward, however, he winked at Shun Wu Koong as the other disciples were filing out of the classroom. Shun Wu Koong could not have been more pleased. He knew that the master had just invited him to a private audience.

At midnight, Shun Wu Koong secretly made his way to the master's quarters and knocked discreetly. That night, he learned the secret of immortality from the master. And as time passed, Shun Wu Koong was taught feats of magic and power. He learned how to fly, change his size, transform himself into other creatures, and control the weather.

The master also taught him a very special trick, which was the secret of self-multiplication. To perform this trick, Shun Wu Koong would pluck a handful of fur from his body and put it in his mouth. He would then chew the fur into tiny particles, which he spat out. As soon as it left his mouth, the fur would turn into thousands of tiny monkeys. Then he would only have to recite a magic spell, and the monkeys would turn back into fur, which Shun Wu Koong would replace on his body.

As he gained power, Shun Wu Koong also became quite vain. He strutted around in front of the other disciples and lorded it over them all. One day, he was showing off his new powers to a crowd of admirers. Hearing the commotion, the old master came out to investigate. When he saw what was happening, he was irate.

"What are you doing?" he thundered at Shun Wu Koong, who had just turned himself into a pine tree.

"I-I-I was just having a little fun," said Shun Wu Koong in a tiny voice, quickly changing back to his original form.

"Fun?! You are not here to have fun! I have misjudged you. I thought you were pure of heart, but obviously you are only a vain little monkey. You can't stay here." Sadly, the old man turned away.

"Please, Master! Don't turn your face away from me. I promise never to show off again. I'm so sorry. Please, please give me another chance and . . ." Shun Wu Koong trailed off helplessly as the master strode back into the cave and shut the door on him.

Because he had no choice, Shun Wu Koong left the Cave of the Slanting Moon and Three Stars. "Oh well, all is not lost. At least I have learned many valuable secrets, including the secret of immortality," he consoled himself. He decided to return to his tribe and set a course for Flower and Fruit Mountain. Because he now could fly, he arrived in a very short time.

"Children, I'm back. Come welcome your king!" Shun Wu Koong shouted triumphantly as he landed. At his call, thousands of monkeys streamed out of every tree and crevice. "Our king is back! Long live the Monkey King! May he live 10,000 years!" they all cried in unison.

"So tell me, what has been happening? Where is the old macaque?" asked Shun Wu Koong when they had all settled down. A wise old ape stepped forward and said, "Dear Monkey King, the old macaque died about ten years ago."

"Died ten years ago! Poor old macaque! Have I really been gone that long?" asked Shun Wu Koong wonderingly.

"Great King, you have been gone for more than twenty years!" said the old ape sadly.

"I can't believe it, twenty years!" marveled Shun Wu Koong. "But my trip was not in vain. I have learned many magical powers and the secret of immortality! I even have a human name now—Shun Wu Koong. It means 'Aware of the Void,' " he boasted proudly.

The monkeys were awestruck at their king's grand new name. That night, they had a feast that lasted for days to celebrate the homecoming of their beloved king and his wonderful new powers.

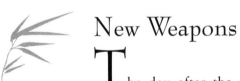

New Weapons

The day after the feast, all the monkeys felt frightfully sick from drinking too much wine, but Shun Wu Koong would not let them rest. He roused them early and made them line up in neat rows. After they were all assembled, he told them that they had lived in idleness for too long. It was high time they learned to defend themselves. He ordered them to train in the art of warfare every day. The monkeys were an unruly bunch unused to discipline, and they groaned until Shun Wu Koong told them that after their exercises were over, they could spend the rest of each day in leisure.

It was soon apparent that the monkeys needed weapons to train with. "But where on earth can we get weapons enough for us all?" mused Shun Wu Koong out loud.

The wise old ape counseled, "Great King, not far east from here is a city full of soldiers. The city arsenal doubtless has enough weapons for us all and more besides."

Shun Wu Koong was delighted. He instantly mounted a cloud and flew to the city of weapons. A high wall constantly patrolled by soldiers surrounded the city. In the early morning light, it looked unassailable indeed. Shun Wu Koong was undaunted. Reciting a magic spell, he caused a great sandstorm to arise. The winds were so strong that everyone ran for cover. Soon, not a soul was left outside. In no time, Shun Wu Koong had forced the doors of the arsenal open. Inside were stacks of swords, bows and quivers full of arrows, armor, spears, axes, catapults, and other weapons. Shun Wu Koong saw that he could not carry them all.

He plucked a handful of fur from his body, chewed it, and spat it out. Soon, thousands of tiny monkeys had cleaned out the arsenal. Shun Wu Koong then said a magic spell, and they all flew on clouds back to Water Curtain Cave, which they reached in less time than it takes to tell.

All the monkeys were soon training with real weapons that very morning. But Shun Wu Koong was still frustrated. He tried all the finest weapons in the arsenal but could find none that satisfied him. "These are all too light, and every single one shatters when I strike it against my leg!" he complained.

The old ape said, "Great King, because you are now so powerful, it is only natural that these weapons are not to your liking. I have heard that the Dragon King of the Eastern Sea has many magical weapons. Perhaps you should pay him a visit."

Shun Wu Koong replied, "What an excellent idea! I can breathe water as easily as air. I am sure that this great Dragon King will be courteous enough to lend me a worthy weapon."

He mounted a cloud and soon reached the Eastern Sea, where he plunged into the water fearlessly. After a little while, he came upon a gorgeous palace of green jade on the bottom of the sea. It was obviously the home of the Dragon King.

A lobster sentry saw Shun Wu Koong approaching. Never having seen a monkey before, the lobster was frightened and hurried into the palace to announce the stranger's arrival. The Dragon King hastily arose to greet his visitor, whom he knew was no ordinary monkey to have traveled underwater as easily as on land.

"Welcome, Immortal," the king said simply, ushering Shun Wu Koong into the palace. After they had taken some refreshment, the Dragon King asked, "So what brings you to my humble home? Surely, you must have a special reason for traveling so far to see me."

Shun Wu Koong lost no time answering. "Great King, I also am a king. Recently, I have been trying to train my subjects in the art of warfare. They are all adequately equipped with weapons, but I can find no weapon to my liking. My most trusted adviser told me that you have many wonderful magical weapons. Surely, there must be one weapon that you wouldn't mind parting with?"

The Dragon King did not want to refuse, for he was famous for his generosity. He quickly ushered the mysterious monkey into his Hall of Weapons, which did indeed contain many deadly and beautiful instruments of war. But none of them appealed to Shun Wu Koong. He hefted one after the other, but all of them were too light. He even broke a few of them against his stone thigh. "I'm so sorry, Great King. I don't really like any of these. They all seem too flimsy."

"Great heavens, too flimsy! Why, that spear you're holding weighs more than 7,000 pounds! Try this battleaxe. It is the heaviest weapon I have. It weighs 10,000 pounds."

Shun Wu Koong hefted the great axe in his hand. It seemed a little better than the others, but when he struck it against his stone leg, the head of the axe shattered into tiny metal shards. When the Dragon King saw this display of power, he shook with fear. He said, "Great Immortal, I have shown you all the weapons I have."

At this point, the Dragon Mother motioned to her son that she wanted a word with him. The Dragon King hurried after her, secretly relieved for a chance to get away. Once they were alone, the venerable old Dragon Mother whispered, "Son, the magic iron rod in our treasury has been glowing for several days. Could this be an omen that we should give it to that stone monkey for a weapon?"

The Dragon King was surprised. "Why, that iron rod was used by the Celestial Ruler to smooth the bottom of the sea. It is too heavy to be moved. What use could he have for a sacred relic like that?"

"I don't know. Just offer it to him and maybe he will go away," said his mother urgently. The Dragon King decided to follow his mother's advice. After all, he had no other options. He hurried back to the Hall of Weapons and told Shun Wu Koong, "Great Immortal, I do have one other special weapon to show you. It is in my treasury."

Shun Wu Koong was delighted. "Well, what are we waiting for? Have it brought here!"

"But it is too heavy to move. I'm afraid we will have to go to the treasury to look at it," replied the Dragon King.

When the doors of the treasury were opened, all were astonished to see a blinding beam of light emanating from the sacred piece of iron. "There it is," said the Dragon King, awestruck.

Boldly, Shun Wu Koong walked forward and laid one hand upon it.

Immediately, the iron rod stopped shining. It was about twenty feet long. "This is too unwieldy. If only it were a bit smaller," he muttered. As he spoke, the iron rod shrank until it was a perfect fit for Shun Wu Koong. He lifted it easily with one hand. "Why, this is perfect!" shouted Shun Wu Koong happily. He struck it against his leg. "Ow!!" he cried in pain, for he had just dented his thigh with the rod.

The Monkey King examined the rod carefully and found that it was as sound as ever. Experimentally, he cried, "Bigger!" The rod grew back to its original size. "Smaller!" barked Shun Wu Koong. The rod shrank and shrank until it was no bigger than a needle, which Shun Wu Koong promptly tucked behind his ear.

He respectfully bowed to the Dragon King, whose mouth was agape, and said, "I don't know how to thank you, Great King."

The Dragon King closed his mouth with a snap. "Don't mention it," he replied stiffly. "I'm glad I was able to help out. May you have a safe journey home."

After many more expressions of gratitude, Shun Wu Koong saw that the Dragon King wished only to be rid of him. Well pleased, the stone monkey mounted a cloud and flew back to the Water Curtain Cave with his newfound weapon.

Shun Wu Koong Visits the Celestial Realm

Because Shun Wu Koong was a good ruler, he held another feast to celebrate the finding of the tribe's new weapons. He knew that his monkeys were a fun-loving people, and he wanted to indulge them. They had a delicious dinner and drank oceans of wine. Shun Wu Koong fell asleep groggily afterwards. He dreamed that the King of the Dead himself appeared before him.

"Come along, stone monkey. Your time is up," said the dreadful monarch.

"Wh-wh-what do you mean? I-I-I am immortal. I have no time," whispered Shun Wu Koong fearfully.

"You are quite mistaken. I have a Register of the Dead, and you are quite plainly listed there. You have already far surpassed the ordinary lifespan of a monkey, even a stone one. Stop wasting time. Come along now," said the King of the Dead.

"Wait!" said Shun Wu Koong more boldly. *"I want to see this register."*

"Very well," sighed the King of the Dead. He took Shun Wu Koong's arm as if they were old friends, and they soon arrived at a great hall where hundreds of clerks were writing with brushes on scrolls. The King of the Dead went to a cabinet marked *"Monkeys"* and pulled out a scroll.

"There, you see?" said the King of the Dead, pointing to the words *"Stone Monkey, 320 years"* with a skeletal finger. On the same scroll, Shun Wu Koong saw descriptions of all his subjects.

By now Shun Wu Koong was no longer afraid. He was angry. *"That's a mistake! I studied immortality with a great master. This scroll is wrong. Here, let me correct it."*

Before the King of the Dead could stop him, Shun Wu Koong grabbed an ink-soaked brush from a clerk passing by and crossed his name out.

Flabbergasted, the King of the Dead protested, *"Are you mad? You can't do that! These names are here by the decree of the Celestial Ruler himself!"* But while he was talking, Shun Wu Koong had crossed out all the names on the scroll.

"Your audacity is unparalleled! I will report you immediately to the Celestial Ruler! He will surely punish you," shouted the King of the Dead. But Shun Wu Koong was already walking away.

The next morning, Shun Wu Koong awoke exhilarated. "Gather round, children! I have great news! We're all immortals!" While the chattering tribe scrambled toward him, Shun Wu Koong told them about his dream.

". . . and then I crossed off all your descriptions too, so now there is no record of us in the Register of the Dead!" he concluded triumphantly.

Of course, this news caused great rejoicing. Every beast on the mountain heard the joyful clamoring of the monkeys and hid fearfully. Another great feast ensued to celebrate the entire tribe's immortality that was even more sumptuous than the one before. This celebration lasted for weeks. In fact, some Chinese say that mountain monkeys seem never to grow old and that these monkeys still fondly remember that great feast so long ago.

Unfortunately, it was just at this time that Shun Wu Koong's existence came to the attention of the Celestial Ruler. The Dragon King of the Eastern Sea had reported the incident of the iron rod to the Celestial Ruler, for he was quite alarmed at Shun Wu Koong's great manifestation of power. Shortly thereafter, the King of the Dead reported Shun Wu Koong's effrontery regarding the Register of the Dead. The Celestial Ruler knew that he had to do something, but he himself was a little intimidated by all he heard.

The Celestial Ruler decided to take an indulgent course with this brazen stone monkey and give him an official post in the Celestial Realm. But the post would not have any real responsibilities attached to it. The wily ruler would instead create a high-flown title for the monkey that would flatter his vanity but give him no real power. And the Celestial Ruler could keep an eye on him.

He summoned Shun Wu Koong to appear before him. "Well, Shun Wu Koong, it seems you have been making quite a name for yourself," he said blandly.

"Oh, well, you know, I was just trying to be a good ruler like yourself," simpered Shun Wu Koong.

"No, no, you are being too modest," the Celestial Ruler protested. "I have heard great things about you. In fact, I have decided that it is time for you to assume an office here in the Celestial Realm. Your title shall be 'Great Sage Equal to Heaven.' "

As the wise ruler predicted, Shun Wu Koong was thrilled with this noble-sounding title. In no time, he was installed in an office and given sumptuous quarters with many servants. But he soon grew bored in the Celestial Realm. There were so many rules! He wandered about all day with no responsibilities and drank copious amounts of celestial wine. Every time his natural curiosity manifested itself, he was told not to bother anyone and to go away. His life grew purposeless.

One day, Shun Wu Koong awoke from a head-splitting hangover and went outside to meander around. He soon came to a lovely peach tree orchard. A beautiful fairy maiden tried to stop him from entering. He appeared to acquiesce, but Shun Wu Koong was tired of all the restrictions. Besides, the huge, golden-red peaches looked irresistible, and peaches were his favorite food. He recited a magic spell that turned him into a tiny monkey no bigger than a mosquito and flew into the nearest tree. There, he gorged himself on the peaches until the entire orchard was bare. They were delicious beyond belief.

After eating the last peach, Shun Wu Koong curled up in a leaf to take a nap. Soon he awoke to the sound of distressed voices.

"All the Peaches of Immortality are gone! Whatever shall we do for the queen's birthday feast?!" cried the lovely fairy who guarded the orchard.

"Oh no! All the most important beings in the Celestial Realm will be there! We can't cancel, the invitations have already been delivered!" wailed another fairy.

Shun Wu Koong overheard this conversation and thought to himself, "Birthday party for the Queen of Heaven? If this birthday party is for the most important people in the Celestial Realm, why wasn't I, the Great Sage Equal to Heaven, invited? It just doesn't make sense."

Then an ugly thought stole upon him. "Wait a minute, maybe this 'Great Sage' stuff is all nonsense. If I am so important, why haven't I been given any duties? All I do is wander around all day.

That Celestial Ruler is just trying to keep me drunk all the time so I won't make any trouble." Shun Wu Koong became extremely angry at the thought that he had been fooled so easily, and he was keenly wounded by his unimportance in his new home. "I'll show them!" he thought. "I'm going to ruin their stupid party, and then they'll take notice of me!"

Shun Wu Koong instantly made himself invisible and flew to the celestial kitchens where the feast was being prepared. Wine stewards were rushing about. "Quick, put that ruby extract here, and make sure that we have enough emerald wine," yelled the head steward.

"Ruby extract and emerald wine! That sounds too good to pass up," said Shun Wu Koong to himself. He recited a spell that put all the wine stewards to sleep. Then he drank up all the barrels of wine and bottles of ruby extract he could find, which was quite a feat given that these delicacies were for one hundred immortals. Indeed, the extract and wine were so delectable that Shun Wu Koong smacked his lips and ruefully left only after the last of it was gone. By now he was frightfully drunk.

Next, he wandered into the kitchen, recited another spell that put all the cooks and serving girls to sleep, and gorged himself. What he could not eat he either spilled on the floor or made unmentionably filthy. By now, he was quite sleepy. He locked all the doors and windows of the celestial kitchens and curled up on the floor to take a nap along with all the other unconscious people there.

Shun Wu Koong awoke to a pounding noise. He was quite refreshed and felt wonderful, for the Peaches of Immortality, ruby extract, and emerald wine were not ordinary food or drink. They fortified him and gave him great strength. Any mortal who had eaten or drunk just a little bit of any of these celestial delicacies would have become an immortal of no small power.

Soldiers summoned by the servants were storming the locked building. When Shun Wu Koong figured this out, he opened the doors and leapt out brandishing his iron rod. He routed all the soldiers in no time and barricaded himself again in the celestial kitchens. The soldiers ran to the Celestial Ruler to report what had happened. The Celestial Ruler was incensed.

"Summon all the troops!! Storm the kitchen! Bring that impudent stone monkey to me for punishment!" he yelled in a terrible voice.

Wave upon wave of soldiers descended upon the celestial kitchens, but they were no match for Shun Wu Koong. He chewed up handful after handful of his fur, and spat out countless tiny monkeys that wreaked havoc among the troops. He also increased his size by magic so that the arrows of the soldiers were no more than pinpricks to him. His great iron rod smashed whole platoons as easily as a flyswatter kills flies.

Helpless, the troops quickly retreated. They told the Celestial Ruler of Shun Wu Koong's great powers and said that they could not defeat the audacious monkey.

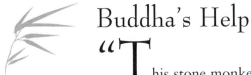

Buddha's Help

"This stone monkey is more powerful than I ever dreamed!" thought the Celestial Ruler. "We need help," he said to his advisers. "Can you think of anyone strong enough to defeat this ape?"

The Celestial Ruler's favorite adviser stepped forward after consulting briefly with the others. "Great Ruler, it's obvious that we need to appeal to someone more powerful than even you," he said humbly.

"More powerful than me? Why, there is only one Being more powerful than me, and that is Buddha himself, the God of Boundless Light!" he said in surprise. His advisers merely nodded.

"I see. Very well, I'll go to Buddha and ask for help," he said. Within the hour, he was standing before Buddha pleading his case.

". . . So as you can see, God of Boundless Light, this monkey has upset the natural order of things and must be stopped," he concluded.

"Yes, I have heard of this stone monkey. It is true that he has broken the rules of the Celestial Realm and earth. I will help you."

The Celestial Ruler was immensely relieved, and they immediately returned to the scene of the fray. Buddha planted himself in front of the celestial kitchens and called out, "Monkey, come out here at once. Your little pranks are at an end."

Shun Wu Koong looked out and saw Buddha, but he thought that Buddha was only a monk, for he had no idea of the existence of such a Being. "What kind of shabby little monk are you that you challenge me, the Great Sage Equal to Heaven?" he taunted.

"And who are you, to think that you can cause chaos in the Celestial Realm and on earth without fear of punishment? Why, you are only a monkey! I'll bet you can't even jump off the palm of my hand!"

Buddha's words angered Shun Wu Koong. "What do you want to bet that I can't jump off your hand?"

"I'll bet the throne of the Celestial Ruler himself," said Buddha calmly. "If you can jump off the palm of my hand, the Celestial Ruler can come and live with me, and you'll take over his throne."

Shun Wu Koong was taken aback that such a humble monk was in a position to offer the throne of the Celestial Ruler himself in a wager. But his pride would not allow him to admit that this monk could best him. He could not refuse this offer. Shun Wu Koong quickly came out. "All right, you're on," he said. "But I feel it fair to warn you that this is only a formality. The celestial throne is as good as mine."

Buddha merely smiled and put down his hand. Shun Wu Koong shrank himself down until he was no bigger than an ant and climbed onto Buddha's palm. As soon as he was at the base of

Buddha's hand near the wrist, he leapt with all his might, growing larger and larger as he did so. He soon reached the greatest size he was capable of and flew for what seemed like an eternity. At last he landed in a place where mist swirled around him. In front of him he saw five immense pink pillars whose tips were lost in the sky.

"Why, I've flown clear to the end of the universe!" thought Shun Wu Koong in amazement. "I'll just leave a little memento of my visit," he chuckled. He squatted down at the base of the largest pillar and relieved himself. He then jauntily saluted the pillars, turned around, and leapt back.

Quite a while later, he landed on Buddha's hand. "See, I've won! I jumped so far that I reached the end of the universe," boasted Shun Wu Koong proudly.

"The end of the universe?!" scoffed Buddha. "Why, you have never even left the palm of my hand!"

Shun Wu Koong was furious. "What are you talking about?! I did fly to the end of the universe. There are five immense pink pillars there, and I left a little souvenir at the base of the thickest pillar."

"You mean this foul pile?" asked Buddha. Shun Wu Koong peered closely at Buddha's hand, and sure enough, his little memento was sending off its pungent fumes at the base of Buddha's middle finger.

Aghast, Shun Wu Koong saw that he had finally met more than his match. He turned to flee, but Buddha merely waved his hand, and Shun Wu Koong was instantly trapped in Wu Shin Mountain near the western entrance of the Celestial Realm. Wu Shin Mountain was made of the five elements of the world: metal, wood, water, fire, and earth.

Buddha appeared before him. "Have no fear. You will not be imprisoned forever. When you fulfill your sentence, one will come who will set you free. He will be my disciple. You must do whatever he asks," he told Shun Wu Koong.

Shun Wu Koong was awestruck at the omnipotence of this Being. As Buddha turned to leave, Shun Wu Koong cried, "Great Immortal, please tell me who you are."

"I am called Buddha, God of Boundless Light," replied Buddha. And he walked away, heedless of the pitiful cries and pleas of the stone monkey.

Shun Wu Koong's Penance

Trapped in Wu Shin Mountain, Shun Wu Koong had plenty of time to think. At first, he despaired. He missed the Water Curtain Cave and his tribe. What good times they had had! He thought about how sweet it was to eat a fresh peach in the morning sun, and he longed for freedom. Then he thought about Buddha, that humble monk who held the entire universe in the palm of his hand. As water wears even the hardest rock down, the stone monkey underwent a gradual change over the centuries thinking about Buddha.

Shun Wu Koong remembered that he had strutted around so vainly and proudly in front of that awesome Being, and Buddha had only smiled. How ashamed Shun Wu Koong was about that now! Then he remembered that he was not to be trapped forever, and he began to have hope. As more centuries passed, Shun Wu Koong began to see how gracious Buddha had been to give him a second chance at freedom.

Buddha hadn't needed to play the hand jumping game with him, the monkey realized. Why, if Buddha had wanted to, he could have immediately trapped Shun Wu Koong forever in Wu Shin Mountain with less than a wave of his hand. The charade of letting Shun Wu Koong try to jump off Buddha's hand must have been done to teach Shun Wu Koong a lesson.

Shun Wu Koong thought about it for a long time and realized that the lesson was this: the truly great have no need for ambition or pride. As he reflected upon these things, Shun Wu Koong felt the deepest respect for Buddha, a god so humble and forgiving, great though he was. It took many more years for him to realize that his respect for Buddha had deepened into another emotion. Thus, Shun Wu Koong learned a second lesson: love. He resolved with all his heart to help Buddha's disciple as Buddha had instructed him, and he waited.

One day, Wu Shin Mountain began to tremble. Shun Wu Koong, who had been sleeping, quickly woke up. A fissure appeared through which the bright sun shone. The crack rapidly expanded until it was big enough for Shun Wu Koong to pass through. When he emerged into the daylight, he found himself before a little monk on a white horse.

"Thank you, Master, for setting me free. I have been trapped in Wu Shin Mountain for 500 years as a punishment for upsetting the forces of earth and the Celestial Realm. Buddha told me that one day his disciple would come and let me out. Tell me, Master, what is your name, and how did you come to be here?"

The little monk was amazed at the sudden appearance of Shun Wu Koong. He said, "Why, I was just passing through and saw this mountain. I was thinking how much easier it would be to go on my way if this mountain wasn't here. Then the mountain began to shake, and here you are. My name is Hsuan Zhang. I am on my way to India to fetch the Buddhist Scriptures from there and bring them back to China. Buddha himself came to me in a dream and told me to teach the people of China the way to enlightenment. What is your name?"

Shun Wu Koong was delighted. "Master, my name is Shun Wu Koong. Buddha told me that I was to obey you without question. He must have meant for me to protect you during your journey west to India and back.

Hsuan Zhang was skeptical. "If you upset the forces of earth and the Celestial Realm, how do I know you're not an evil monster? You could be tricking me in order to kill me and steal my horse."

Shun Wu Koong laughed. "Master, if I had wanted to, I could have killed you as easily as look at you. If you don't believe me, watch this." Shun Wu Koong then grew as tall as Wu Shin Mountain and took his iron rod from behind his ear. "Bigger!" he commanded, and the rod expanded until it was proportional to Shun Wu Koong's great size. He lifted the rod over his head and smashed Wu Shin Mountain to pieces.

Terrified, Hsuan Zhang knelt in the dust and prayed to Buddha. Seeing that he had frightened the poor little monk, Shun Wu Koong quickly shrank back down to his usual size. "Sorry, Master. Please don't be afraid. I just wanted to prove to you that I mean you no harm. When I was trapped, I had a lot of time to think about things, and I now regret the folly of my ways. I have resolved to seek the path of enlightenment by learning Buddha's way."

Hsuan Zhang thought, "Surely, what this monkey says is true. He could easily have killed me. Perhaps Buddha really did mean for this creature to protect me on my journey west. After all, who could ask for a better bodyguard? Also, I could probably teach this monkey much about Buddha's way." Aloud he said, "Very well, Shun Wu Koong. I agree that Buddha must have meant for us to travel together on this quest. Come, let us be on our way."

Shun Wu Koong's Desertion

Shun Wu Koong and Hsuan Zhang traveled well together. Shun Wu Koong told the monk many entertaining stories about his past history. In return, Hsuan Zhang taught the monkey much about Buddha. Shun Wu Koong was grateful for this gentle and patient instruction. He could not wait to prove himself worthy to serve as Hsuan Zhang's companion on the road to India.

One day, they were walking along as usual when six men armed with axes and swords rushed out at them and quickly surrounded the two travelers. Their leader, a huge ruffian with a thick black beard, demanded, "You there, hand us over your travel packs and the horse."

Hsuan Zhang said to Shun Wu Koong, "Do as he says."

"What?! Are you mad? They want to rob us, and then after we hand over our things, they'll certainly kill us so we don't report them to the provincial officials. I'll deal with them."

Before Hsuan Zhang could protest, Shun Wu Koong faced the leader and said, "Why don't we make a little deal? It's obvious that you've done this sort of thing before. If you hand over one-seventh of your booty to us, we will go on our way without killing you. That way, we can all share equally in your ill-gotten wealth. You'd also be helping two disciples of Buddha, so you'd be doing your immortal souls a big favor."

At this suggestion, the robbers laughed so hard that tears rolled down their cheeks. The leader said, "Monkey, you've got nerve, that's for sure. Now stop fooling around and hand over your things before we kill you. That way we won't get your blood all over the loot."

Shun Wu Koong was outraged. He took out his iron rod and slew all six of the bandits.

Hsuan Zhang was horrified. "Shun Wu Koong, why did you kill them all? Haven't you learned anything about Buddha or his way? He teaches gentleness and forbearance. Surely you know this by now!"

"But Master, they would have killed us! I was only trying to be a good bodyguard," replied Shun Wu Koong, stunned.

"Surely you are powerful enough to have merely disabled them. Why, you could have put them to sleep as you did the staff of the celestial kitchens. Instead you have killed them. Now they can never achieve any degree of enlightenment in this life," said Hsuan Zhang mildly.

Although Shun Wu Koong had indeed learned much about enlightenment, this remark stung him to the heart. His amazement turned to anger, for he could not stand criticism.

"Fine, if that's the way you feel about it! I'll go on my way by myself. I could go back to the Water Curtain Cave and be the Monkey King again," he retorted.

Hsuan Zhang said nothing, which further enraged Shun Wu Koong. Without another word, he gathered his things together and walked away.

Sadly, Hsuan Zhang said to himself, "Well, I guess I wasn't meant to have a disciple help me on my journey after all." And he went on his way alone.

At nightfall, Hsuan Zhang saw an old woman by the side of the road. She said, "Little monk, where are you going?"

"To India," he replied.

"Surely you don't expect to reach that distant land all by yourself! You'll probably get yourself killed long before you even reach the western lands of China," she said with surprise.

"Well, I did have a disciple, but he behaved badly. When I scolded him, he left in a fit of temper," replied Hsuan Zhang.

Hsuan Zhang did not know that the old woman was really the Goddess of Mercy, Kuan Yin. Buddha had sent her to help the monk. She said, "I have here a magic cap. If your disciple comes back to you, make him wear it. He will not be able to take it off once it's on. If he disobeys you, merely recite this spell." She whispered the spell in Hsuan Zhang's ear. "He will not disobey you then. When he has truly become enlightened, the cap will fall off his head by itself."

The old woman then led him to a little shack, fed him a simple meal, and made him a bed of straw to sleep on for the night. Hsuan Zhang gratefully collapsed and immediately fell asleep.

Shun Wu Koong's Return

Meanwhile, Shun Wu Koong set out for Water Curtain Cave. On the way, he decided to visit the Dragon King of the Eastern Sea again. From afar, the same old lobster sentry saw Shun Wu Koong approaching the jade palace and quickly announced him. The Dragon King was a bit fearful of seeing Shun Wu Koong again.

"Why, what are you doing here, Great Immortal? It's been a long time. Listen, I'm sorry about your imprisonment. I . . ." he began, trying to excuse himself.

Shun Wu Koong cut him off. "Oh, don't worry about that. I know you reported me to the Celestial Ruler. It's quite all right. I've learned a lot about myself and even became a disciple of Buddha for a little while. Now I'm on my way back to the Water Curtain Cave."

"A disciple of Buddha?! What happened? Why did you stop?" asked the Dragon King in surprise.

Shun Wu Koong replied, "My master was too impractical. He got mad at me because I killed some bandits. They would have killed us, but he got angry and told me I hadn't learned enough about Buddha's way."

Thoughtfully, the Dragon King replied, "Great Immortal, maybe your master was right. After all, to become enlightened, you must learn patience and gentleness. You have not shown your master that you have either quality. Remember when you first visited my palace? We were all terrified of you. Power and ruthlessness were written all over your face."

Shun Wu Koong said nothing but appeared to be deep in thought. Finally, he said, "Great King, thank you for your generosity, which I will never forget. I feel as if you and I are old friends now. I have decided to return to my master. Your wise words changed my mind. Thank you for everything!" Without another word, Shun Wu Koong disappeared, leaving the Dragon King shaking his head in wonder at the great change in the capricious ape he had known so long ago.

In no time, Shun Wu Koong had traveled back to the spot where he had killed the six bandits. He searched in vain for Hsuan Zhang, but all he found was the old woman. When he asked if she had seen Hsuan Zhang, she led him to her hut.

Shun Wu Koong quickly walked inside and awakened the monk. Kneeling by the bed, Shun Wu Koong said, "Master, I'm so sorry I deserted you. I will never leave your side again!" He all but wept as he finished this speech.

"I'm touched by your loyalty, but I don't know if I can ever trust you again," replied Hsuan Zhang. "I have here a cap. If you really mean to accompany me all the way to India, you must wear it."

Shun Wu Koong did not know that the cap was magic. He quickly donned it, happy to have been forgiven so easily.

Experimentally, Hsuan Zhang recited the spell the old woman taught him. Shun Wu Koong immediately clutched his head as if red hot needles were being inserted into his skull. He writhed on the ground in agony.

Hsuan Zhang could not bear to see his disciple in such pain and stopped the magic. Shun Wu Koong suddenly sat up. To be on the safe side, Hsuan Zhang tested the spell again. Shun Wu Koong instantly dropped to the ground in extreme pain, trying in vain to wrench the cap off. Hsuan Zhang stopped reciting.

Shun Wu Koong was bewildered. "Master, what is this cap? It hurts my head, and I can't seem to take it off."

"Ah," said Hsuan Zhang sadly. "I'm sorry, Shun Wu Koong. It's a magic cap that the old woman gave me. Whenever you disobey me, I need only recite a spell to put you in extreme pain. Fortunately, when you have become truly enlightened, the cap will fall off by itself."

Shun Wu Koong could see Buddha's hand in this. He dared not become angry. Instead, he humbly said, "Master, I understand that Buddha in his wisdom does not feel that I am worthy yet to accompany you on the way to India unless I wear this cap. I see now that I was cruel when I slew those bandits. As you know, I still have a lot to learn. I will try to defer to your wisdom in the future, and maybe you will not have to use the cap spell as often as time goes by. Some day, I hope that the cap will fall off by itself when I become truly enlightened."

Hsuan Zhang was pleased at this change in Shun Wu Koong. He clasped the monkey's paw warmly, and they immediately became the best of friends again.

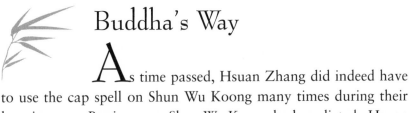

Buddha's Way

As time passed, Hsuan Zhang did indeed have to use the cap spell on Shun Wu Koong many times during their long journey. But it was as Shun Wu Koong had predicted. Hsuan Zhang needed it less and less. Shun Wu Koong gradually learned the qualities of gentleness and kindness. He slowly learned not to be vain or needlessly cruel. And these lessons he learned through experience, with his heart and not just his head.

Now, whenever the travelers were threatened or witnessed evil, Shun Wu Koong used his power to imprison the evildoers or compel them to do some good deed in the name of Buddha instead of killing them. For his part, Hsuan Zhang gently tried to teach these wrongdoers the righteousness of Buddha's way. Many of them thought about their pasts and repented of their ways in much the same way Shun Wu Koong had while he was trapped in Wu Shin Mountain. In this way, the two disciples of Buddha set many on the path to enlightenment.

They finally reached India, where they retrieved many scrolls of Buddha's Scriptures before beginning the long trip back. They had countless adventures, and it would take up an entire book by itself to tell of all they encountered.

One day, the travelers neared the spot where Wu Shin Mountain had originally been located. It was seventeen years since their fateful meeting. Instead of becoming more familiar, however, the landscape became increasingly unearthly. The trees, grass, and flowers shimmered with a strange, beautiful light. Within a few days, the travelers reached a compound of many buildings with yellow eaves that shone like topazes in the sunlight. Shun Wu Koong realized that they had reached Buddha's palace.

Hsuan Zhang excitedly sprang down from his horse. A young monk quickly came out of the temple to greet them. "Master is expecting you," he told them simply. He led them to the Great Hall, where Buddha himself was seated.

Shun Wu Koong and Hsuan Zhang quickly threw themselves down in front of their beloved god. Smiling, Buddha bade them to rise. "In all the great land of China, the people lived in ignorance of my way. Greed, lust, pride, and all the vices of mankind have ruled the land. Now because of your journey to the west, the way to enlightenment will be made clear to the people. They will learn many of the same lessons you have, Shun Wu Koong, such as gentleness and forbearance. They will strive to do good."

Buddha bade the young monk to take the holy scrolls of Scripture from Hsuan Zhang. "These will be given as a present to the Emperor of China, who will recognize that they define a great new religion. He will see to it that this religion is introduced to the Chinese people," Buddha said.

Although he was overjoyed to be in Buddha's presence again, Shun Wu Koong also felt unaccountably sad. He looked over at Hsuan Zhang and saw that the little monk was also downcast. "What is wrong with us? Buddha has just praised us, and yet we are unhappy," thought Shun Wu Koong. Then he realized that he felt very empty inside. He and Hsuan Zhang had indeed completed a great mission, but now they had no reason to live. Their purpose in life was gone.

Shun Wu Koong addressed Buddha, "God of Boundless Light, we were glad to be of service and honored beyond words that you deigned to choose us as the instruments of your will. But what are we to do now? We would like to be of more service to you. It is the only thing that will make us happy again."

Buddha merely smiled. Suddenly, Shun Wu Koong felt his head curiously, for something was different. The magic cap had disappeared. "Now that you are free, do you want to change your mind? I will understand if you do," said Buddha gently.

Shun Wu Koong thought about his tribe at the Water Curtain Cave and the freedom that he had there. But he also thought about the pointlessness of his life there, where his whole existence had been only a pursuit of comfort for himself and his tribe. In fact, he was just as imprisoned by this pursuit of comfort as he had been by the magic cap. His love for Buddha, who had given him a purpose in life, overwhelmed him the next moment.

Shun Wu Koong smiled back at Buddha and said, "I want to serve you BECAUSE I am free."

Shun Wu Koong had at last achieved perfect enlightenment. Buddha replied, "Well said, my child. Because it is your wish, I appoint you to serve me as the God Victorious in Conflict. This post should perfectly suit you because you are never happier than when you are facing opposition. The appointment is also fitting from a spiritual standpoint because no one knows better than you how difficult it is to triumph over one's own weaknesses. You will defend the weak and helpless who are in need of a champion and inspire the spiritually weak to overcome their faults."

Next Buddha turned to Hsuan Zhang and said, "You have done a great deed worthy of merit. Because of this, I appoint you to serve me as the God of Merit. You will aid and encourage those who, like you, undertake difficult tasks to achieve enlightenment."

Buddha descended from his seat and held out his hands. Joyfully, the two newly appointed gods stepped forward, and each took hold of one of his hands. Together, they walked forth into the bright sunlight.

過而能改
善莫大焉

"No virtue is greater than reforming one's faults." —Tzo Ch'iu Ming (sixth to fifth century BC), from *The Commentary of Tzo*. Translated by Shelley Fu.

Notes on
Journey to the West

This story uniquely combines elements of fantasy, mythology, religion, satire, and history. The fantastic and mythological elements of the story are obvious in the figure of Shun Wu Koong himself, one of the most beloved of all Chinese characters. He is often portrayed wearing a skirt made of a tiger skin, one of the first creatures he killed, as a symbol of his prowess.

The Chinese view monkeys much as Westerners do—they are regarded as unruly and comical. Shun Wu Koong's transformation from an unruly monkey to a disciple of Buddha who learns to use his powers constructively symbolizes the power of faith and of Buddha. In a way, Shun Wu Koong is the opposite of Lucifer, the fallen angel of the Bible. Shun Wu Koong begins his spiritual journey in a fallen state and ends up being deified as his pride and vanity are humbled.

Shun Wu Koong's journey to India is more trying as a spiritual journey than a physical one. He becomes an Everyman, or pilgrim, whose struggles symbolize common man's striving toward spiritual perfection. His transformation also can be taken to symbolize the change for the better (according to the story) of the Chinese people as they embraced Buddhism.

On a satirical level, the story gently mocks the hierarchy evident in the Celestial Realm. This hierarchy mirrors the actual political hierarchy in China during the T'ang Dynasty.

Shun Wu Koong's rebellion against those above him may embody the resentment of the Chinese peasant class against the aristocracy.

On a historical level, Hsuan Zhang is a real figure, a monk of the T'ang Dynasty, who did indeed travel to India to retrieve the Buddhist Scriptures. He lived in the seventh century. Many believe that he is the greatest translator in Chinese history for the numerous sutras he translated from Sanskrit. The importance of his journey cannot be underestimated, for he was responsible for making Buddhism popular in China.

In fact, many Chinese converted to Buddhism during the first half of the sixth century, when Liang Wu Di, the Emperor of China, endorsed it in a public speech. One hundred years later, when Hsuan Zhang returned from India with the scrolls of sutras and began the tremendous task of translating them (AD 645), Buddhism reached its highest point of influence in China. It is therefore natural that the story of Hsuan Zhang's journey would be embellished into the realm of the fantastic.

With the introduction of Buddhism, the hierarchy of Chinese gods changed drastically. Before Buddhism, Taoism was the prevalent Chinese religion. Under the Taoist hierarchy, the Celestial Ruler is the emperor of the celestial court, as he is in "Ho Yi the Archer." However, the gods and monsters outside of the Celestial Ruler's court could be much stronger. That is why even the Celestial Ruler fears Shun Wu Koong, who refuses to acknowledge the emperor's jurisdiction. Older gods such as Pan Gu and Nu Wo predate both Taoism and Buddhism. They also seem to have powers that surpass those of the Celestial Ruler.

With the advent of Buddhism, the celestial hierarchy was modified to include Buddha and his helpers, such as Kuan Yin, the Goddess of Mercy, and the God Victorious in Conflict and the God of Merit, the posts that Shun Wu Koong and Hjuan Zhang fill. Buddha himself is supposed to be the most powerful being in the universe. Of course, this is from a Buddhist point of view, and "Journey to the West," which was written to promote Buddhism, would naturally support it.

Wu Cheng En, who lived in the sixteenth century, wrote the most famous version of this story. Before his rendition, the "Journey to the West" was a folktale passed on orally by storytellers. It is ironic that before he authored this story, Wu Cheng En was an obscure writer of little account who wrote only in classical Chinese (*wen yen wen*) in a very scholarly vein. In contrast, he decided late in life to record the "Journey to the West" in colloquial Chinese (*bai hua*) much the way it would have been told by storytellers in the teahouses of the Sung Dynasty (AD 960 to 1279). Today, very little of Wu Cheng En's classical Chinese poetry remains, but he is extremely well known for his wonderful and detailed account of the "Journey to the West."

The Man
in the Moon

吳
剛
伐
桂

Long ago, there was a village in China by the banks of the Yellow River. It was a very poor village, and everyone who lived there was always on the verge of starvation because floods from the river would devastate the crops. One year, the famine was particularly bad because the river had flooded three times, and no one had enough to eat.

During this time of privation, a little boy from the village was working in his family's field one day when he spotted a tiny sparrow with a broken wing hopping around on the ground. He approached the sparrow slowly and picked it up. It shook uncontrollably, and its tiny heart was racing.

"Please don't be afraid. I will not harm you. I am only trying to help," he said soothingly.

The sparrow seemed to calm down at the little boy's kind words. The boy took the sparrow home and carefully bound its wing. Then he put it in a cage and fed it food with his own hands from his meager meals until its wing healed. When the sparrow was well again, the boy opened the cage door and let it fly free.

"Goodbye little bird! May you fly strongly until the end of your days," he called after it, waving and smiling.

Later that day as he was at work in the field again, a sparrow flew fearlessly up to him and landed at his feet.

"Why, you look just like the little bird I just rescued! Could it be that you're the same sparrow?" he asked wonderingly.

The sparrow did not reply but dropped a tiny seed at the little boy's feet. The boy picked up the seed and examined it, but finding it of no value, he threw it away. The sparrow flew after the seed and again deposited it at his feet. Again he threw it away, and again the sparrow retrieved it. This happened three times.

Amazed, he asked, "Little sparrow, why do you persist in giving me this seed? Is it that you want me to plant it?"

The sparrow actually seemed to nod. Deep in thought, the little boy pocketed the seed. Apparently satisfied, the sparrow flew away.

Later that day, he told his parents what had happened. His mother said, "Son, perhaps the sparrow you rescued is an immortal in disguise. He has rewarded your thoughtfulness with this seed. You must plant it so as not to anger the immortal."

His father agreed, saying, "Yes, you must plant it in the garden behind our hut. Nurture the shoot that will sprout from the seed as lovingly as you cared for the bird that brought you this gift."

The little boy did as his parents said. Every day before he went to the fields, he watered the tiny sprout, and it soon grew into a mighty vine with branches as thick as his leg. Strangely enough, the plant did not yield one single fruit.

He asked his parents, "Should I continue to nurture this plant? It has not borne any fruit and is choking all the other plants in the garden to death!"

His father agreed. "Yes, it seems to be a waste of time. Maybe you should kill the plant. Then we can dry it out and use it as fuel in our stove."

The mother disagreed. "Son, you will anger the gods if you do not care for this plant. We will wait until the end of summer. If it still has not yielded any fruit, we can destroy it then."

The family agreed that this was a reasonable solution, even though it had dire consequences on their small income from selling the produce from their garden. Months passed in this way, and still the boy faithfully watered the plant every day. Finally, just as the family was deciding to kill it, the plant bore a single, tiny green gourd. The gourd rapidly grew bigger and bigger and more golden every day until it was as large as the little boy himself. The family then decided to harvest it.

"What a lot of soup this fine fruit will make! We could feed the whole family for months on its bounty!" his parents rejoiced.

The little boy took his ax and went into the garden. He chopped the gourd from the vine and then cut into the fruit. Immediately, a shower of gold and precious gems spilled out. The immense gourd contained enough riches to ensure the family's fortune for generations.

"We're rich! Rich beyond our wildest dreams!" the family rejoiced. Their happiness was so great that they cried with joy. They took their treasure and headed for the capital, where they bought a fine mansion and lived together in prosperity and comfort.

By this time, the entire village had heard the story of the miraculous gourd and the kind-hearted little boy. Most people were happy for the family, for they were good people and never begrudged anyone in need. One little boy, however, was very unhappy whenever he heard the story. His name was Wu Gan.

"Why did that sniveling little brat come into such a fortune? We're starving and have to work from sunup until sundown in the fields, mucking around in the mud, and we can't even eat a decent meal after all that toil. I never could stand that do-good little snob. Why should he have it so easy?" Wu Gan thought to himself. He nurtured his envy until it turned into great hatred for the rich family. His discontent grew until he could not even sleep well at night.

One day as Wu Gan was out working in the fields, he spotted a sparrow in a tree not far from him. He picked up a rock and threw it half-heartedly at the sparrow, but he missed. It was then that he came up with a plan. He immediately dropped his hoe and raced off.

"Where do you think you're going?! Come back immediately! You're not done harvesting your portion of the field!" his father yelled after him.

Wu Gan ignored him and quickly ran home, where he immediately set up a small paper lantern in a tree. Every day, he would practice throwing rocks at the lantern. His parents berated him for his strange new hobby.

"Why don't you help us anymore in the fields? We need you to help us with the harvest! Without your help, we'll starve," his mother admonished him.

"So what? We're already starving," retorted Wu Gan.

"How will your throwing rocks at a paper lantern help the family?" his father asked angrily. "Hard work is the surest way to riches."

Wu Gan replied smugly, "We've worked liked slaves our entire lives, and it's gotten us nothing. I have a plan. When the time comes, you'll understand everything."

His parents saw that they could not dissuade him and left him alone. After about a month, Wu Gan could hit the paper lantern with a rock every time on the first try. He then picked up his hat and headed for the fields. Soon, he spotted a sparrow. He picked up a nearby rock and threw it at the sparrow. It fell from the tree at once. Wu Gan ran up to the little bird and saw that he had broken its wing.

"Perfect!" he exulted. He took the sparrow home and tended it as carefully as the other little boy had. In time, the poor bird healed.

Wu Gan said to it, "I have nursed you back to health. Now you must bring me a reward. If you don't, I'll throw rocks at every sparrow I see and leave them to die. Chances are you'll be one of these birds." He then opened the door of the cage, and the sparrow quickly flew away.

Later that day, just as Wu Gan had planned, the sparrow reappeared. It landed at his feet, where it dropped a large round seed. "If I plant this, will I be rewarded with great riches?" asked Wu Gan. The sparrow seemed to wink and flew away.

Like the other little boy, Wu Gan planted the seed in the family garden and tended the little sprout until it too grew into a mighty vine. In time, it also bore a single gourd that grew as huge as the first one. It had exactly the same rich golden color as the other gourd. The family was ecstatic.

"Let's harvest it tomorrow," the father decided.

"Yes, and then we will be so rich we won't know how to spend the money," his mother gloated.

"And we'll never have to see this miserable village again!" added Wu Gan.

That night, Wu Gan was hard-pressed to fall asleep. He kept thinking about the fine new mansion, clothes, and grand carriage he would buy with the money, as well as the countless servants he would hire to wait on him. However, the thought that he had to share the wealth with his family rankled him.

"I won't give any to the family," he thought. "After all, they complained incessantly and never lifted a finger to help. I'll get up in a couple of hours before the sun comes up and reap my harvest. I could make it to the capital by sundown," he decided.

Just as he was thinking this, sleep overcame him, and he dreamed about an old man with a beautiful white beard and flowing white hair. The old man had a huge jar of sweets, but the opening of the jar was very small.

"You may help yourself to a treat, but only one," he said to Wu Gan.

Wu Gan's eyes opened as big as saucers at this windfall. He reached his hand deep into the jar and grabbed as many sweets as his hand could hold. Unfortunately, when he tried to withdraw his fist from the jar, the opening wasn't big enough. The only way he could remove his hand was to let go of all the treats he had grabbed except one. This he was not willing to do. He stubbornly tried to pull his fistful of treats out again and again, panting and desperate.

"Cruel and foolish boy, your greed will get you nothing!" said the old man in disgust. With these words, both the old man and the jar full of sweets disappeared.

Wu Gan awoke bathed in sweat. He thought, "If I go into the garden now and cut the gourd open, I can grab all the riches and be in the city before the family wakes up and keep it all to myself! How lucky it was that that horrible dream awakened me in time!"

He took his bag and an ax and sneaked into the garden soundlessly. His hands were trembling with excitement as he took the ax to the gourd. He hacked and hacked, but no jewels or gold came pouring out. Finally, the gourd split open, and an old man emerged. Wu Gan rubbed his eyes in disbelief, for it seemed to be the same old man who had visited him in his dream. Fear sent an icy chill down Wu Gan's back, and his hair stood on end. He cowered before the majestic old man, faint with fear.

"I have come to give you your reward," said the old man.

At these words, Wu Gan's fear evaporated. He straightened up and said, "It's about time. What's it going to be? Gold? Jewels? Come on, hurry up! I've waited forever!"

"I will show you riches no mortal has ever dreamed of," replied the old man. "Grab your ax and bag, and take hold of my hand."

Boldly, Wu Gan stepped forward and did as he was told. As soon as he took the old man's hand, they began ascending into the air. Higher and higher they flew until Wu Gan's breath failed him. He was again filled with fear.

"Where are we going, old man?" he managed to squeak out.

"We are going to the moon," was the reply.

After a while, they did reach the moon. Wu Gan saw that all the mountains and trees were made out of silver. He couldn't believe his eyes. He also saw a beautiful lady wandering about, but he did not want to stop and talk to her. All he wanted was to receive his treasure and get back to earth. He immediately ran up to a massive silver boulder and began hacking at it with his ax, trying to break off a piece.

"Stop that!" barked the old man irritably. "I have something much better to show you. Follow me," said the old man.

Wu Gan eagerly obeyed. They walked for a few minutes until they reached a magnificent tree. Its trunk was of precious, polished cassia wood, and each leaf was exquisitely sculpted of the finest, deep green jade. The tree also bore a dazzling array of fruits of every color, each one a perfect gem of enormous size. There were sparkling diamonds, sapphires, pearls, rubies, and fire opals. The tree was so splendid that it glowed with its own light.

At the sight of this unearthly beauty, Wu Gan's pulse quickened, and the blood rushed through his veins.

He barely heard the old man say, "This is your reward!"

"W-what did you say? Y-y-you mean, I c-can have it?" Wu Gan couldn't believe his ears.

"If you can chop this tree down with your ax, it is yours. You can put it in your bag, and I will take you back to the human realm," chuckled the old man.

Wu Gan didn't notice the twinkle of mischief in the old man's eyes. He purposefully approached the tree with his ax and took a mighty swing at the base of its trunk. Almost immediately, the cut he had made healed over. Wu Gan was flabbergasted. He dropped his ax and bent down to examine the tree trunk. It looked as sound as ever. He ran his hand over the place where the cut should have been. It was as good as new! There was not even a small nick in the polished, gleaming wood.

Wu Gan began frantically hacking away at the tree at a furious pace. Wood chips flew everywhere. But each cut he made immediately healed over, and he got nowhere. He tried to shake the tree to dislodge the precious jewels, but they were securely attached to the tree. Try as he might, he could not even pluck the smallest of the jewels from the tree. The old man looked on with a sardonic smile, not saying a word. Wu Gan took up his ax and again tried desperately to chop down the tree.

Finally, the old man spoke. "Greedy boy! You will never be able to chop down this tree! It is your punishment to stay here until you can control your greed. Only then can you return to the human world and resume your life."

Wu Gan was so preoccupied that he did not hear these words or see the old man disappear into thin air. He had eyes only for the tree trunk and ears only for the rhythmic sound of his ax as it bit into the rich red wood. Wu Gan stayed by the tree all night at his futile task.

In the morning, the beautiful woman he had seen approached him. "Oh, thank goodness you are here! I am Tsang-O. I have been stranded here alone for longer than I can remember. I used to live on earth, like you. I am so very lonely. Please, please put down your ax and talk to me!" she pleaded with tears in her lovely eyes.

Wu Gan didn't even lift his gaze from his task despite the woman's breathtaking beauty. He was dead to everything but the tree. Hesitantly but desperately, Tsang-O plucked at Wu Gan's sleeve. Wu Gan turned toward her for the first time.

Enraged, he roared, "Leave me alone! Can't you see I am trying to cut down this tree?! I have to cut it down so I can be rich. I'll be richer than the emperor! It's my reward."

Suddenly, an ugly suspicion entered Wu Gan's head and his eyes narrowed. "Did you hear me? Go away! You can't have any. It's all mine!" He approached her menacingly, wielding his ax.

Terrified, Tsang-O ran away. Wu Gan turned back to his exhausting task with new vigor.

"You can't chop that tree down, it's magic," Tsang-O called to him from a safe distance. "Why don't you put down your ax, and we can keep each other company. We are the only two people in this forsaken place!" she wailed. Wu Gan did not hear her. Tsang-O finally gave up and wandered sadly away across the cold silver landscape.

As time passed, Wu Gan began to age, but he is doomed never to die. It has been thousands of years since his adventure began. The Chinese believe that Wu Gan is still there, hacking away at the magic tree, a wizened old man now with a snow-white beard. On a clear night when the full moon is out, perhaps you can see him swinging away.

善惡到頭終有報
只爭來早與來遲

"Good will eventually be rewarded and evil punished; it's just a matter of time." —Hsih Nai-An (AD fourteenth century), from *Water Margin*. Translated by Shelley Fu.

Notes on
The Man in the Moon

This story is a Chinese parallel of the Greek Sisyphus myth. Like Sisyphus, Wu Gan is doomed to forever repeat a monotonous and unending task. Unlike Sisyphus, Wu Gan dooms himself to this hell by his own unceasing greed. Similar to Aesop's fables, many Chinese tales have a moral aspect to them that discourages bad behavior. The moral nature of this and other Chinese stories reflects Buddhist, Confucian, and Taoist teachings.

Wu Gan's blindness and deafness to all else but wealth indicates that he has no self-knowledge—he is unaware of his own faults despite the obvious warnings he is given (his dream and the old man's behavior). According to the Buddhists, this is a great sin because only those with self-knowledge can seek enlightenment. From a Confucian standpoint, his disobedience and planned desertion of his family is unforgivable. Finally, according to Taoist teachings, man and nature should live in harmony. Thus his cruel treatment of the sparrow cannot go unpunished.

This story also explains the markings on the moon and correlates to the ancient Chinese belief that the moon is a cold, lonely, and unforgiving place. Some versions of the story include a cock or rabbit that attacks Wu Gan as soon as he ceases to chop at the cassia (or cinnamon) tree. One of the earliest renditions of this story is in Duan Chen Tse's *Miscellaneous Topics from You Yang* written some time during the ninth century (T'ang Dynasty).

TALES
OF LOVE

愛情

The Story of the White Snake

白
蛇
傳

Two Snakes

In the western part of China was a famous mountain called O Mei Mountain. From base to top, it was over 3,000 meters tall. The top of the mountain was very cold even in summer. Much of the mountain was covered with virgin forest and had no roads. After August, the mountain became too cold to climb. Besides those training for immortality, only birds and beasts lived here.

In a cave on the mountain lived two snakes, a big white snake and a small green one. These snakes were no ordinary snakes. The white snake had already been training for immortality for one thousand years and the green snake for slightly less long. Their training allowed them to take on human form or any other form, and they had many magic powers. They were close to attaining enough enlightenment to become gods. Occasionally, they would come out of the cave and wander the mountain.

"Life on this mountain is really boring!" The green snake finally voiced its discontent one day.

"We are in training and can't change our lives now," the white snake warned.

"Who cares if we achieve godhood if the life of a god is this dull?"

"Do you wish to go to the human realm?" asked the white snake with surprise. Although they had never visited the human realm, they had heard of its glamor and excitement.

"If human life is as happy as they say," the green snake replied.

"But the happiness is only temporary."

"Maybe, but the happiness is much more intense than the happiness of immortality."

The white snake was skeptical and did not reply. They had had this discussion many times over the years, but it had never gone any further.

One day, the green snake hit upon a new idea. "Why don't we go to the human realm and take a look, then come back? It won't affect our training to make a quick visit," suggested the green snake. The white snake did not reply.

The green snake pestered the white snake for many years, and the white snake finally said, "If I were to visit the human realm, I could change myself into a beautiful maiden, the fairest in the human realm."

"I could change into your pretty little servant girl," the green snake said happily.

The white snake uttered some magic words, and in no time, they changed into two lovely human maidens. The maiden that was the white snake named herself Bai Su-Tzin, for *bai* means "white" in Chinese. Her servant girl chose the name Shao Chin, which means "Little Green."

Bai Su-Tzin was so pleased with her new form and pretty name that she lost all reservations about visiting the human realm. "Let's go to Jiang Lan, south of the Yangtze River," Bai Su-Tzin said, gaining conviction.

"Yes, yes! Jiang Lan is the most flourishing and prosperous place in China!" Shao Chin was so excited that she was on the verge of tears. "We can finally see the famous West Lake."

The Human Realm

In March, West Lake in Jiang Lan was at its most beautiful. The weather was warm, the sky was blue, white clouds floated by, and the ground was covered with green grass and red flowers. Truly, West Lake was gorgeous, with its banks covered with weeping willows and blossoming peach trees. The swallows had just returned from the south and flew amongst the willow trees gaily. People dressed in beautiful clothes walked about or rowed boats upon the lake, drinking wine and singing.

Suddenly, an exquisite young woman dressed in white appeared on shore. Her clothes floated around her, stirred by the breeze. She seemed to have descended from the sky. "She is as beautiful as a fairy," everyone whispered. "She is so radiant she can't be mortal. Look! She has a maid, and even her maid is as fair as the sky."

Bai Su-Tzin's and Shao Chin's appearance caused everyone to stop and stare at them. This gave Bai Su-Tzin a strange feeling she had never had before—a feeling of triumph. It was as if they had conquered everyone by their beauty. "The human realm is too good to be true. How can a life of training for godhood on a cold mountain compare to this?" Bai Su-Tzin softly asked Shao Chin, basking in the looks of admiration from all sides.

"We were wise to come," replied Shao Chin. "If we had known earlier how good this life was, we would not have wasted so much time trying to become gods."

In the crowd, a handsome young man carrying an umbrella was walking rapidly along. Although he saw Bai Su-Tzin and Shao Chin, he didn't stop to stare but hurried along with a preoccupied air.

"What a strange young man," said Shao Chin to Bai Su-Tzin. "It's as if he didn't see us." She was annoyed.

"He must be a gentleman," said Bai Su-Tzin.

"A gentleman?! I can't believe that. He must be an idiot. The weather is superb, and he's carrying an umbrella!" Shao Chin replied.

"Let's think of an excuse to talk to him."

"Excuse? Well, maybe if it began to rain . . ."

"Rain? Excellent! Let it rain." Bai Su-Tzin uttered a magic formula, and suddenly black clouds appeared and rain began to fall. Everyone by the lake ran for cover. Only the young man remained calm. He opened his umbrella and walked to the edge of the lake to rent a boat.

"Excuse me, young master," called Shao Chin to the young man. "My mistress is over there," she said, indicating Bai Su-Tzin, who was standing under a tree. "We came out without bringing an umbrella. May we ride on the boat with you?"

"Um, of . . . of . . . of course." It seemed as if the young man had never spoken to a woman before, and he stammered and turned red as a peony. Bai Su-Tzin and Shao Chin daintily climbed aboard, and the youth had no choice but to sit directly opposite Bai Su-Tzin in the cramped cabin. He was extremely agitated and kept looking out the window.

"What is young master's name?" asked Bai Su-Tzin.

"M-m-my . . . my name is Shu Shen. I. . . I'm from Zhen Jiang."

Bai Su-Tzin proceeded to ask Shu Shen many questions. Although he was nervous and kept stammering, she learned that

his father and mother died long ago and that his younger sister was married and lived in Soochow. He now lived alone. Despite his scholarly appearance, Shu Shen was not a student. His family was very poor, and they had no money to send him to school. He worked in a pharmacy as a clerk.

"Young miss, what is your name?" Shu Shen inquired shyly. He seemed to relax a little bit.

"I am Bai Su-Tzin. I come from Sichuan Province. My father and mother are also deceased. My father was once a government official . . ." Bai Su-Tzin made up a convincing story of her past.

When the boat reached the other side of the lake, it was still raining. Shu Shen gallantly offered them the use of his umbrella. Bai Su-Tzin promised to return the umbrella the next day, but Shu Shen refused. Instead, he proposed to pick it up at their house.

"That's a good idea," said Bai Su-Tzin, pleased at his gentlemanly offer. "I also live not far from here. Go east about one mile, and you'll see my house, which has red gates. Please come visit us tomorrow."

When they were alone, Bai Su-Tzin said to Shao Chin, "Now we need a house." Near the lake, they found a broken-down temple. It was deserted and very dilapidated. Bai Su-Tzin uttered a magic formula, and the temple was immediately transformed into a beautiful house with red gates.

Meanwhile, Shu Shen thought over the day's events. He had never met such a beautiful woman before. She was generous and dignified, as well as amiable. Bai Su-Tzin had treated him, a poor pharmacy clerk, as if he were an equal. Their meeting seemed so fortuitous. Shu Shen thought that the Celestial Ruler must have planned it, for the night before he had dreamed that it would rain. "Thank goodness I paid attention to the dream and brought an umbrella! It must be that fate has a hand in this," said Shu Shen to himself as he walked home.

The Visit

Shu Shen did not sleep at all that night. The afternoon finally arrived, and he set out for Bai Su-Tzin's house. From afar, he could see it. It was huge! Its gates were vermilion, and a high wall surrounded it. "I should turn back," thought Shu Shen. "Her servants will never let me in." At that moment, the gates opened, and out came Shao Chin.

"Master Shu, you're here! Why don't you come in?" asked Shao Chin amicably.

Inside the gates, the house was even more impressive. It had a big courtyard filled with trees. Everything was beautifully and tastefully arranged. All kinds of flowers grew in the gardens, and fountains sparkled in the sunlight as water flowed into small ponds filled with colorful carp. Bai Su-Tzin was awaiting him at the end of the courtyard.

"Please come in, Master Shu," she said with a smile. She was even more beautiful than the day before.

Bai Su-Tzin's house was furnished richly and artistically. "Such a lovely maid, such beautiful surroundings, this must be heaven," Shu Shen said to himself.

Bai Su-Tzin invited him to sit down, and Shao Chin immediately entered with dish after dish of delicacies and wine. The aroma of the delicious food was irresistible, and Shu Shen ate quite a lot. After a few glasses of wine, he felt more at ease, and his tongue loosened. As they drank more and more wine, they conversed more and more easily.

Bai Su-Tzin asked Shu Shen what his plans were for the future. He replied that he wanted to run his own pharmacy some day but that it was a difficult thing for a poor clerk like himself to do. "If I had money, it would be a different story. I would know exactly what to do," he asserted.

They drank wine and talked until nightfall. It grew dark outside, but Shu Shen made no move to leave. Bai Su-Tzin didn't seem to want him to go, and Shao Chin became uneasy. "Master Shu, please drink some tea now. Our mistress has to change her clothes," said Shao Chin, darting a meaningful look at Bai Su-Tzin.

When they were alone, Shao Chin scolded, "It's not early anymore. We should ask him to leave."

"Leave? Why don't we ask him to live here instead?" asked Bai Su-Tzin. "I want to marry him."

"Marry him?! How could you do that?" Shao Chin was alarmed. "We are only here temporarily. Besides, there are so many young men in the world. Why do you want to marry a poor pharmacy clerk?"

"I think I love him."

"But if we stay here, we will never attain godhood. Besides, why don't you look around some more? He's the first man you've met!"

"Please, Shao Chin, I need your help," Bai Su-Tzin coaxed. "I fell in love with Shu Shen at first sight, and I can't help myself. If you don't want to help me, I understand, but I have no choice. I was meant to be with him. You can go back to O Mei Mountain if you want, but I will miss you terribly," Bai Su-Tzin concluded, clasping Shao Chin's hands.

Shao Chin was moved. She knew that the ascetic life on the mountain would be unbearable without Bai Su-Tzin. After all, they had been companions for many centuries. "I'll do all I can to help you," she promised finally and went out alone to talk to Shu Shen.

"I'm sorry, Master Shu. My mistress must rest for a while."

"Oh! It's late, and I should be going." Shu Shen stood up as he suddenly realized that it was dark outside.

"Don't worry," said Shao Chin. "Mistress asks you not to leave. She needs to talk to you about something. Master Shu, are you engaged?" Shao Chin wasted no time getting to the point.

"N-no, not yet," he stuttered nervously.

"Well, why can't I be your matchmaker?" asked Shao Chin jokingly.

"Matchmaker?! Who would you set me up with?"

"Why, with my mistress of course!"

"Your mistress?" Shu Shen blinked in surprise. "How could I marry her? She would never consider me, a poor clerk."

"You are mistaken. All along, mistress has been looking for an honest young man like you to marry," lied Shao Chin.

Shu Shen could not believe his luck.

The Pharmacy in Zhen Jiang

After Bai Su-Tzin and Shu Shen had been married for a short while, they decided to move to Zhen Jiang so that Shu Shen could open his own pharmacy. Zhen Jiang was a big, bustling city on the southern bank of the Yangtze, not far east from where Nanking is today. Bai Su-Tzin pretended that she was a wealthy orphan whose inheritance was more than enough to help Shu Shen fulfill his dream. In reality, she and Shao Chin used magic to steal money from wealthy families. They never stole too much from one house, so the thefts were rarely noticed. In no time at all, Shao Chin and Bai Su-Tzin had stolen a small fortune. In the busiest part of town, they bought a building. They lived upstairs and ran the store downstairs.

Strangely enough, everyone who bought medicine from Shu Shen's pharmacy completely recovered from sickness. Bai Su-Tzin herself examined the customers who came in. Even though Zhen Jiang was a big city, it had no female doctor, especially such a beautiful one. Not only that, but Bai Su-Tzin cured patients no other doctor could cure. People soon beat a path to their door to get examined and buy medicine. Business was booming. The God of Fortune himself seemed to be looking after Shu Shen. It was not long before Bai Su-Tzin became pregnant. Even Shu Shen couldn't believe his luck. He had a beautiful wife, a beautiful maid, coffers filled with gold, and now he was a soon-to-be father!

But nothing good on earth stays that way forever. Other pharmacists, jealous of Shu Shen, spread a rumor. "That Bai Su-Tzin is probably an evil monster," they said. "How could such a beautiful female doctor be mortal?"

The rumors spread and spread until they finally reached even the Gold Mountain Monastery, a famous monastery south of Zhen Jiang on a high mountain. It was a massive complex with red roof tiles and yellow walls. Thousands of monks lived there. How many, no one knew. But one thing was certain—all the monks there had achieved a high degree of learning and spiritual training. The abbot's name was Fa Hai, and his level of spiritual training was so high that no one knew the full extent of his powers.

When Fa Hai heard the rumor about Bai Su-Tzin, he was indignant. How dare an evil monster live so close to their monastery? Such contempt! He felt that he had to investigate and expose Bai Su-Tzin's masquerade.

One morning, the pharmacy was doing business as usual, and people were lined up outside to buy medicine. Suddenly, an old monk appeared at the door. He was very tall and had snow white hair. He didn't say a word but stared intently at Bai Su-Tzin, who was examining customers. Shu Shen had just come downstairs, and the monk looked piercingly at him as well.

"I am the abbot of Gold Mountain Monastery, Fa Hai. Young Master, let's go somewhere quiet and talk," he said to Shu Shen.

"Master Shu, I was walking by your pharmacy and saw the aura of evil spirits, but you do not have that aura," said Fa Hai once they were seated in Shu Shen's office.

"But Master Fa Hai, where are these evil spirits you speak of?"

"The evil spirit is with you all day! It is your wife! I just saw her."

"Master Fa Hai, please don't joke around about my wife." Shu Shen was very unhappy. Not only did he love Bai Su-Tzin, he respected her.

"Great Buddha! How could you be so blind? The Dragon Boat Festival is approaching. On that day, let your wife drink too much wine. Then you will believe me," said Fa Hai, and he got up to go without so much as saying goodbye.

The Dragon Boat Festival

The Dragon Boat Festival was on the fifth day of May, just as summer began. Because the weather was warming up, people believed that poisonous insects and snakes came out of their winter hibernation. That is why on that day, people drank Shung Hwang wine. This special wine contains sulfur and was said to kill or sicken poisonous creatures and cure their bites. All poisonous creatures therefore feared sulfur.

Because the day of the festival was approaching and Shun Hwang wine would be everywhere, Bai Su-Tzin and Shao Chin had to plan what they would do. Shao Chin suggested going to the mountains for the day to hide.

"I can't. If master doesn't see me every day, he's sure to be anxious," Bai Su-Tzin said.

"Then what are we to do? On that day, the odor of sulfur will be everywhere. I won't be able to stand it," said Shao Chin.

"You go up to the mountains by yourself," said Bai Su-Tzin. "I'll stay here with my husband. It should be no problem. I have one thousand years of training. I think I'll be able to stand it."

The day of the Dragon Boat Festival finally arrived. Every household made food and wine for picnics at the dragon boat races, which were held on the Yangtze River. Shao Chin had left for the mountains the day before, where she found a cave. She prepared to rest for a day. That morning, Bai Su-Tzin said that she wasn't feeling well and wanted to stay in bed. Shu Shen came in quite often to check on her.

The clerks at the pharmacy had prepared a feast, and Shu Shen sat with them drinking. He suddenly thought about Fa Hai's advice. "How could that monk think my wife is an evil monster? He must have been spouting nonsense. I'll bring her a little wine," thought Shu Shen to himself drunkenly. With a large glass of Shung Hwang wine in each hand, Shu Shen staggered upstairs and into Bai Su-Tzin's room.

"Wife, come. A toast to you," said Shu Shen loudly.

"I can't drink wine right now," Bai Su-Tzin replied. "You know I don't feel well today."

"You caught a bit of a cold. Drinking a little wine would do you good. Besides, today's a festival. Everyone should be happy." Shu Shen seemed a bit angry.

"I should be able to stand one glass," Bai Su-Tzin thought to herself. "All right," she said. "I'll join you for one glass, but just one glass." Shu Shen toasted his wife, and they drank together.

"Why don't you sleep? I'm leaving, but I'll be back soon." So saying, Shu Shen wove his way downstairs. "That monk really cannot be believed," he said to himself.

The taste of sulfur made Bai Su-Tzin very uncomfortable. She got an unbearable headache and felt nauseated but tired. She fell asleep. And as she slept, slowly she lost her human beauty and turned back into a big white snake!

After their feast, the pharmacy clerks went to the river to see the boat races. Shu Shen didn't want to leave his wife, so he didn't go. He drank more but felt lonely, so he lumbered upstairs again. "Are you asleep? I'll lay down next to you," said Shu Shen drunkenly, getting into bed. He put his arm around the lump in bed next to him. It felt funny, so he drew back the sheets.

When he saw the big white snake snuggled in bed with him, Shu Shen was so scared that he couldn't breathe, and his heart beat so violently he felt that it would burst. "Snake!" he finally managed to yell. Shu Shen fell out of bed, scared literally to death.

The sun was setting when Shao Chin returned. The pharmacy was unusually quiet. "The clerks are probably still out," thought Shao Chin. She went upstairs and found Shu Shen lying on the floor, dead.

"Mistress!" Shao Chin called Bai Su-Tzin.

Bai Su-Tzin awoke, and when she saw Shu Shen lying on the floor, she screamed. "My husband! I shouldn't have had that glass of wine! What are we going to do? Can we save him?" She began to cry helplessly.

"He's not breathing," said Shao Chin regretfully. "Unless you go to the Spirit of the West and get the elixir of immortality, he can't be saved."

"The elixir of immortality? Yes, I'll go to Kun Lun Mountain!" cried Bai Su-Tzin.

"But what if the Spirit of the West won't give you any? It only gives such a gift to human mortals, and very few at that." Shao Chin was skeptical.

"Then I'll steal it," said Bai Su-Tzin desperately.

"Steal it?! No! No one has ever done that before. It's too dangerous. Don't go!" pleaded Shao Chin.

But Bai Su-Tzin had made up her mind to save her husband, no matter how dangerous it was. She loved Shu Shen so much she would even go to Kun Lun Mountain for his sake. With the elixir of immortality, Bai Su-Tzin and Shao Chin could be gods because they were already so close to attaining immortality, but Bai Su-Tzin didn't even think of this. All she wanted was to save Shu Shen.

"If I don't return in three days, I'm dead for sure. You can then return to O Mei Mountain alone," said Bai Su-Tzin, clasping Shao Chin's hand.

"You'll come back, Mistress, you'll come back! May the gods protect you," said Shao Chin, weeping.

Kun Lun Mountain

Bai Su-Tzin rode a cloud to Kun Lun Mountain and thus reached it very quickly. She began to ascend the mountain. After a while, she had almost reached the river near its top.

"Halt!" roared a voice like thunder. "What kind of puny snake spirit is it that dares come to Kun Lun Mountain?" In front of Bai Su-Tzin a god as tall as a three-story house materialized. Its appearance was truly ferocious. It had a green face, red hair, and teeth the size of a man's head. Its eyes, which were as big as balls and bulged from its face, immediately saw through Bai Su-Tzin's disguise.

"I . . . I am from O Mei Mountain. I . . . I humbly b-b-beg the Spirit of the West for the elixir of immortality." Bai Su-Tzin was so scared she could only stutter.

"HA, HA, HA!" The ferocious spirit opened its huge mouth and laughed uproariously. "A little snake spirit like you comes to Kun Lun Mountain to steal the elixir of immortality from the Spirit of the West. HA, HA! That's rich!" It seemed the spirit could read minds as well.

Bai Su-Tzin knew this spirit was not about to let her pass. She quickly pulled out her sword and stabbed it, but it was so big that she only injured its leg. The spirit was not seriously wounded at all, but it was extremely incensed at Bai Su-Tzin. It reached out one huge hand and took the sword from her as easily as one takes a toy from a baby. With its other hand, it grabbed hold of Bai Su-Tzin and lifted her to its face.

After looking at her closely, it shook its head, saying, "Too small for a meal, but enough for a snack." The spirit raised Bai Su-Tzin to its open mouth.

"You must not harm her," said a voice behind them. It was a friendly-looking old lady. She seemed harmless, with her white hair tied neatly in a bun, her face wrinkled. But the ferocious

spirit was terrified of the old lady and set Bai Su-Tzin gently on the ground.

"The elixir of immortality is only supposed to be given to humans," said the old lady to Bai Su-Tzin. "But your love for your husband has touched the Celestial Ruler. He has ordered me to give you what you ask for. I will give you enough elixir for one person." The old lady handed Bai Su-Tzin a package. "Give this elixir to your husband, and he will come back from the dead."

"Th-th-thank you," Bai Su-Tzin said, throwing herself at the old lady's feet. She was too overcome to say more and dared not ask the old lady if she was really the Spirit of the West in disguise. Tears of grateful thanks streamed down her face.

Shu Shen's Doubts

The elixir from Kun Lun Mountain was truly miraculous. When Bai Su-Tzin put it in Shu Shen's mouth, his heart immediately started beating and he began breathing again. Although Shu Shen didn't wake up, he slept peacefully for a whole day. The next day he awoke as from a nightmare. He remembered having a bad dream . . . something about a snake. He looked around. Everything seemed so peaceful and normal, and Bai Su-Tzin was sleeping next to him as usual.

"Strange, such a horrible dream, but . . . ." Shu Shen was very uneasy and decided to avoid his wife. That day, he worked like a slave in the pharmacy. When night fell, he told Bai Su-Tzin that there was too much work to be done and that he would sleep in his study. Bai Su-Tzin and Shao Chin knew that this was an excuse, but what could they say? Day after day passed, and Shu Shen never returned upstairs. After about a week, Bai Su-Tzin felt that something had to be done. She prepared food and wine and asked Shao Chin to invite Shu Shen upstairs.

"Tell your mistress that I'm very busy. I don't have time to eat," Shu Shen told Shao Chin in an icy tone.

"Mistress has gone to a lot of trouble preparing a feast for you," said Shao Chin a bit angrily. "You haven't come upstairs for a week. Are you really that busy?"

Shu Shen's face turned red. He knew he looked like he was lying. He couldn't very well refuse without causing a scene. Shao Chin finally got him upstairs. Everything seemed back to normal. Bai Su-Tzin drank wine and talked.

"Su-Tzin, you shouldn't drink wine," Shu Shen said fearfully.

"It's only one glass," said Bai Su-Tzin laughingly.

"But the day of the Dragon Boat Festival . . ."

"Oh, that day I wasn't feeling well. Are you still angry about that?" Bai Su-Tzin joked.

Behind Shu Shen's back, Shao Chin threw a white ribbon out of the window into the yard. She uttered a magic formula, and the ribbon turned into a big white snake. Then she made a point of looking out the window.

"Snake! Snake!" Shao Chin screamed, pretending to be scared.

"Where?" Shu Shen ran to the window. "That's it! That's the snake that lay in your bed on the day of the Dragon Boat Festival!" said Shu Shen.

"Kill it! Hurry up and kill it," cried Shao Chin.

"Don't harm it," said Bai Su-Tzin calmly. "It could be a dragon in disguise. The ancient books say that in the sky, dragons have a dragon shape. When they come to earth, they assume the form of a snake. Think about it, a snake this size should be in a mountain cave. How could it have gotten to Zhen Jiang, a big city? It's probably a dragon that likes our house and has decided to live here. The next thunderstorm, it will fly back into the sky."

Bai Su-Tzin didn't want the snake to be killed because it would turn back into a ribbon. So she pretended to have read this in the ancient books. Shu Shen was not very well read. He wasn't clear about what the ancient books say. But he remembered hearing of dragons and snakes as a boy, and what he heard agreed with Bai Su-Tzin's theory.

A sense of relief flooded through Shu Shen. He really wanted to believe her. "You're right, wife. You're entirely right," he agreed.

"It has already lived at our house for many days," continued Bai Su-Tzin. "On the day of the Dragon Boat Festival, it came into my room. I was scared to death and immediately ran downstairs to find someone."

"Oh, so that's what happened! I saw it lying on your bed. I thought that . . ." Shu Shen was very embarrassed. "It's all that monk's lies. He's contemptible!" Shu Shen blamed Fa Hai.

"What monk?" asked Bai Su-Tzin and Shao Chin simultaneously.

"The old monk that came to the pharmacy a few days ago from Gold Mountain Monastery. He's the abbot. He told me you were an evil spirit, wife." Shu Shen told the whole story.

Bai Su-Tzin lowered her head and didn't speak. Tears fell down her cheeks. Shu Shen was miserable for doubting her. He should have trusted her. Who was Fa Hai anyway? He didn't know him, whereas Bai Su-Tzin was the woman he loved. She looked more beautiful than ever to him. He had almost lost her through his foolish doubts!

"I'm so stupid! How could I accuse my own wife of being an evil monster? Wife, please don't be angry. This is all that mangy monk's fault! I'll never see him again," swore Shu Shen.

Thus, peace was restored in their home.

Gold Mountain Monastery

In no time, autumn had arrived. One day, Shu Shen had business that took him to an area near Gold Mountain Monastery. After his meeting, he wandered around. Near the mighty Yangtze River, the wild grass had turned yellow. Far away, Gold Mountain was covered with trees whose leaves had turned yellow and crimson. Nearby, the red rooftops of many houses were visible.

"Long time no see, young Master. Do you have time to visit our monastery today?" Shu Shen turned around to see Fa Hai standing behind him. "It is very close," said Fa Hai, pointing to the rooftops.

"Maybe another time. I can't go today," replied Shu Shen distrustfully.

"Gold Mountain Monastery is the biggest monastery in this region of China! Why not go take a look?" asked Fa Hai.

"He's right. Gold Mountain Monastery is so famous. Why shouldn't I just go take a look? It couldn't do any harm. Fa Hai is being so friendly. If I don't go, I'm sure to offend him," thought Shu Shen to himself.

"Well, all right. But I can't stay long," said Shu Shen.

Gold Mountain Monastery was truly huge. Its high surrounding walls enclosed countless houses. Without a guide, a visitor would never be able to find the way out. Fa Hai was extremely amiable and invited Shu Shen for tea and snacks. Eventually, the conversation turned to Bai Su-Tzin, the subject closest to both their hearts.

"Young Master, didn't the events on the day of the Dragon Boat Festival prove that I was right?"

"Oh, that day I was scared almost to death," said Shu Shen.

"You now know that she's an evil monster. Why do you still live with her?" asked Fa Hai.

"Monster? No, you're mistaken." Shu Shen didn't want to talk about it.

"The snake you saw that day was her. She's a snake spirit. Even her servant girl is."

"You're wrong. It was a dragon, like the ancient books say," said Shu Shen, thinking of Bai Su-Tzin's words.

"Master, your love blinds you. Dragons live in the sky or ocean. They don't live around here. That day, because your wife drank Shung Hwang wine, she transformed into her original shape. Men and spirits should not live together."

"I don't believe you. Su-Tzin and Shao Chin have been very good to me. They've never done me any harm. How could they be evil monsters?"

"Maybe what you say has been true so far, but it's hard to know what they'll do in the future. Spirits and men don't think the same. What if they get angry with you some day?"

Shu Shen was very troubled and didn't say anything for a long time. "What do you think I should do?" he finally asked.

"Stay here for a while. We can protect you," suggested Fa Hai.

Shu Shen was very unhappy, but because he was afraid, too, he took the monk's advice. "After all," he reasoned, "it couldn't hurt." That night, Shu Shen didn't return home.

Three days passed in this way. Bai Su-Tzin was frantic and sent the pharmacy clerks everywhere to ask for news of Shu Shen. Finally, a clerk returned and told them that people had seen Shu Shen with a monk, and they had walked toward Gold Mountain Monastery together.

"Gold Mountain Monastery!" Bai Su-Tzin and Shao Chin exclaimed together. "That meddling monk Fa Hai must have lured him," said Bai Su-Tzin.

"But Master said he wouldn't talk to that monk again," said Shao Chin angrily.

"We'll go to Gold Mountain Monastery to find him," decided Bai Su-Tzin.

"What if Fa Hai won't let Master go?" asked Shao Chin.

"Then I'll kill Fa Hai!" said Bai Su-Tzin with determination. "I'll kill all the monks in Gold Mountain Monastery if I have to."

"Good. We'll kill Shu Shen too and then return to O Mei Mountain," said Shao Chin happily. She felt that this was the solution to all their problems.

"No! My husband is a good man," Bai Su-Tzin retorted. She still loved Shu Shen deeply.

"Mistress, stop deluding yourself!" replied Shao Chin, exasperated. "He's cowardly and untrustworthy. He doesn't deserve your love. Why should we give up our chance at achieving godhood for him? You treat him so well, but he . . ."

"Don't say another word, Shao Chin," warned Bai Su-Tzin. She would not discuss the matter anymore. "We'll leave immediately."

The Battle at Gold Mountain Monastery

Gold Mountain Monastery was normally a very busy place, with thousands of worshippers visiting the temple every day. On this morning, two new visitors arrived: a woman dressed in white and her maid dressed in green. Both were armed with swords and loudly demanded to see Fa Hai. But all the monks were also prepared, for each one was armed. They drove the worshippers away, and although the monastery was quiet, tension was in the air.

"The monastery welcomes you," said a monk, motioning the women in. When they entered, they encountered Fa Hai with his cane, surrounded by armed monks.

"Fa Hai, where have you hidden my husband?" demanded Bai Su-Tzin.

"Shu Shen is here, but he doesn't want to return with you," Fa Hai calmly replied.

"I don't believe you! Let him come out here and tell me so himself!"

"No. Man and spirits should not mix. He doesn't see you for what you are. You should both return to O Mei Mountain immediately."

"That's nobody's business but our own. You can't control us!" Bai Su-Tzin said angrily. She and Shao Chin drew their swords and advanced.

"This is Gold Mountain Monastery. How dare you show such contempt!" Fa Hai raised his cane to parry their swords. On all sides, the monks drew their weapons, and a great battle began. Bai Su-Tzin and Shao Chin had studied swordsmanship, and even though they were outnumbered, they were unafraid. Suddenly, Fa Hai hit Bai Su-Tzin's sword with his cane, and the cane broke. The monk hadn't expected Bai Su-Tzin to be so formidable. He quickly retreated. Bai Su-Tzin would have followed him, but battling monks surrounded her on all sides.

"Let's go," yelled Shao Chin above the din of the battle. "They are too many. We must retreat and think of a plan."

"But I must find my husband," shouted Bai Su-Tzin, unwilling to relent.

"With this many houses and this many monks, where are we going to look?" Shao Chin shouted back. Bai Su-Tzin realized she had no idea, so she joined Shao Chin in flight to the Yangtze River, where they could think and plan.

"How are we to battle so many monks?" Shao Chin asked breathlessly when they got there. She wanted to go home.

"We can't just give up," disagreed Bai Su-Tzin.

"If we could find some troops to help us . . ." said Shao Chin, thinking hard.

"Wait! That's it! The water spirits of the Yangtze!" Bai Su-Tzin was staring at the mighty river. "They could help us!" She muttered some magic words, and the water started bubbling as if in a great cauldron. Soon countless water spirits came in reply to her summons. Huge fish, shrimp, crab, shellfish, turtle, and eel spirits surfaced. They all listened to Bai Su-Tzin's request, but many were unable to leave the water and couldn't ascend Gold Mountain.

"Fine, then I'll bring the waters of the Yangtze to the monastery doors!" Bai Su-Tzin intoned another magic formula, and the waters of the Yangtze began to rise in huge waves, wave upon wave, until they reached the gates of Gold Mountain Monastery and beat down the great doors. The mighty water spirits swarmed into the monastery, weapons raised. They fell upon the monks under Bai Su-Tzin's orders. Crab generals and shrimp commanders led the attack.

The water spirits were trained in warfare and drilled frequently. When victorious, they often devoured their defeated opponents. The monks were clearly outclassed, and the battle turned quickly. But just when the monks were on the verge of defeat, Bai Su-Tzin suddenly fainted. She was very ill because of her advanced pregnancy. Without her as their general, chaos immediately began in the ranks of the water spirits. The monks rallied for a counterattack, and the unorganized troops of water spirits began to suffer defeat after defeat.

The waters on Gold Mountain retreated back to the Yangtze as the water spirits fled in all directions. Shao Chin, protecting the unconscious Bai Su-Tzin, also retreated until once again they reached the shores of the river.

"Where should we go?" Shao Chin asked herself. "We can't go back to Zhen Jiang, where that monk will find us. Let us go to Soochow."

Soochow

The monks of the Gold Mountain Monastery felt that they had won a great victory. They all discussed the events of the battle. Shu Shen asked every monk he met about his wife, "Please, sir, what happened to my wife?" But none of them knew.

"I've got to leave here and find her. I should never have listened to Fa Hai," Shu Shen said softly to himself. He secretly left the monastery and returned to the pharmacy, but Bai Su-Tzin was not there. Shu Shen roamed everywhere looking for her for weeks. All happiness had fled along with his wife. Finally, he realized that things couldn't go on in this way.

"I'll go to live with my sister in Soochow," Shu Shen made up his mind. He sold the pharmacy and boarded a boat to Soochow. It was already night when the boat arrived. Shu Shen could make out two women on the shore. They seemed very familiar.

"Bai Su-Tzin! Is that you?" Shu Shen excitedly began to yell and leapt ashore as soon as the boat neared land.

"Husband! Could it be?" a low and weak voice responded.

"Bai Su-Tzin! Su-Tzin!" Shu Shen ran quickly to her and then saw Shao Chin. She was holding a sword and stood in front of Bai Su-Tzin. Her expression was cold. Shu Shen tried to get near his wife, but Shao Chin leveled her sword at him. Shu Shen was stunned.

"Shao Chin, have you gone mad?" he asked.

"Don't come any nearer!" Shao Chin was mad enough to kill him. "Our mistress treated you so well, and still you run to the Gold Mountain Monastery to hide." Shao Chin advanced step by step toward Shu Shen.

"I . . . I . . . Su-Tzin!" Shu Shen was so anxious he didn't know what to do.

"Shao Chin! Come back here. How could you be so rude to Master?" Bai Su-Tzin's voice was commanding, but as soon as she said these words, she collapsed. Shao Chin dropped the sword and ran to Bai Su-Tzin's side, with Shu Shen on her heels.

"It's nothing. I just need to rest for a bit, then I'll be better," Bai Su-Tzin said softly. To Shao Chin, she said, "You mustn't blame Master."

Shu Shen took control of the situation. "We can't stay here. We'll go to my sister's house," he decided.

That night in Soochow, Bai Su-Tzin bore a son. With a child, any house becomes warmer. All resentments were water under the bridge, and harmony was restored. Shu Shen's life in Soochow was extremely comfortable. He was rich and had no need to work. His sister, wife, and Shao Chin managed household affairs beautifully. Day after day passed pleasantly in this way, but a storm was brewing.

Although the monks at the Gold Mountain Monastery thought of the battle with Bai Su-Tzin as a great victory, Fa Hai was not satisfied. "Those two snake spirits are too powerful. They actually commanded the water spirits of the Yangtze to battle with me!" he thought. "Although we won the battle, we couldn't kill them. They shouldn't be allowed to carry on their charade in the human realm any longer."

The Golden Alms Bowl

Fa Hai knew that his own powers were insufficient to defeat Bai Su-Tzin and Shao Chin, so he went to Lin Mountain, where Buddha himself lived. Fa Hai hoped to steal a magical gold alms bowl from Buddha. Although this was dangerous, he was obsessed with defeating Bai Su-Tzin and Shao Chin.

Usually, an alms bowl is a very ordinary implement that every monk uses to beg. But the one that Fa Hai hoped to steal was very special. It could be used to trap spirits, no matter how powerful. Fa Hai turned himself into a large turtle and hid under Buddha's seat for many days. Finally one day, Buddha dozed off. Fa Hai left his hiding place and turned himself back into a monk. He stole the golden alms bowl and then fled back to the human realm.

Fa Hai then watched Shu Shen's house for days disguised as a peddler. When he saw Shu Shen leave, he blew on the gold alms bowl and then on a tray filled with strings. The bowl turned into a gorgeous gold crown studded with jewels, and the strings turned into beautiful and ornate gold bracelets. Fa Hai approached the house and knocked on the door.

When Shao Chin opened the door, Fa Hai said, "I have some beautiful wares to sell. Jewelry and hair combs – everything a lady desires." He uncovered the tray of exquisite bracelets. "May I see the lady of the house?"

The jewelry dazzled Shao Chin. "Just a minute, I'll see if the mistresses are available." She ran to get Bai Su-Tzin and Shu Shen's sister. When all four were seated, Fa Hai brought out the tray of bracelets. Bai Su-Tzin and Shu Shen's sister were just about to try a couple of them on when Fa Hai pulled the crown out from under his robe. The three women gasped at its beauty.

"A lovely lady such as yourself deserves the best," said Fa Hai to Bai Su-Tzin. "You are the only one I've seen who is beautiful enough to wear it. Its beauty would overwhelm the face of any other," Fa Hai smiled unctuously.

As soon as Bai saw the crown, she had to have it. "Why don't you try it on?" coaxed Fa Hai. He stood up to place the crown on her head. Bai Su-Tzin made no move to stop him. But once the crown was on her head, it grew tighter and tighter. She tried to pull it off, but it wouldn't budge. The pain was unbearable, and she fell to the floor in a faint. Shao Chin and Shu Shen's sister ran to help her when Fa Hai threw off his disguise.

"You!" yelled Shao Chin.

Fa Hai sneered at Shao Chin and the prone Bai Su-Tzin. "You are in my power now. You'll never live in the human realm again!" Then he blew on the crown, which changed back into the alms bowl. It rolled off Bai Su-Tzin's head and began to emit a blinding white light. The beams of light covered Bai Su-Tzin and Shao Chin, and they started to shrink. They shrank and shrank until they turned into two snakes, which Fa Hai gathered into the bowl. Shu Shen's sister was too stunned to move, and Fa Hai quickly fled from the house.

When Shu Shen returned home, neither Shao Chin nor Bai Su-Tzin were there. His son was crying loudly. His sister was sitting on the floor gazing fixedly ahead with bulging eyes. She didn't seem to recognize anyone. The house was a mess, as if a great struggle had taken place. "What happened?! Where are Bai Su-Tzin and Shao Chin?" Shu Shen asked anxiously.

His sister began crying. "I was scared to death!" she said between sobs. "A . . . a monk . . . came here . . ." She told him the whole story.

"Fa Hai! It had to be Fa Hai . . ." Shu Shen was so overcome that he collapsed. It was a long time before he woke up to see a doctor bending over him while his sister looked on worriedly.

Shu Shen never saw Bai Su-Tzin or Shao Chin again. As the years passed, Shu Shen felt as if his entire life with Bai Su-Tzin and Shao Chin had been a dream—a beautiful dream that was a little scary, too. Despite his fear, he felt as if he had lost something unspeakably wondrous, and life seemed empty and meaningless. He wanted to die, but he couldn't. He still had his son to think of—his poor, motherless boy.

Thunder Hill Pagoda

In Soochow, the story of the two snakes spread. It was said that Fa Hai had buried the bowl with the two snakes in it under Thunder Hill Pagoda, outside of Soochow by West Lake. Legend has it that the pagoda was built around the year 900. In Shu Shen's day, it had a long history and was already very dilapidated. But when the evening sun set, its reflection would be cast into West Lake, and the pagoda still looked beautiful indeed. Many famous poets and painters went to Thunder Hill Pagoda for inspiration.

When Shu Shen heard that the two snake spirits were rumored to be buried under the pagoda, he often went there hoping to find Fa Hai's gold alms bowl or a white or green snake. He never found either, to his immense regret. Time passed, and Shu Shen's son grew up rapidly. Every year on the day of Bai Su-Tzin's disappearance, Shu Shen took his son to Thunder Hill Pagoda. He often stared at the pagoda for hours, as if it was a rich source of happy memories for him. Shu Shen's son never saw his father smile except on the days they went there.

"Father, why are we here?" Shu Shen's son would ask.

"Well, when your mother died, she was buried under this pagoda," Shu Shen would reply. Over the years, he had fabricated a complex story about Bai Su-Tzin and Shao Chin. The real story was too unbelievable, and he couldn't tell it to his son.

Many centuries after Shu Shen's death, Thunder Hill Pagoda collapsed. Some people said that the two snake spirits used magic to escape the gold alms bowl. Others said that the Celestial Ruler felt sorry for the two snake spirits, who, after all, had committed no evil deeds, so he set them free.

Over the years, most people slowly forgot about Thunder Hill Pagoda and the story of the snakes. Occasionally however, an old person will sit on the bank of West Lake in front of a group of children and tell them a story—a story about a white snake and a green snake.

願得有心人
白首不相離

"I wish to marry one who shares my feelings,
So we can stay together until our hair turns white."
— Anonymous (second to first century BC), from *White Hair.*
Translated by Shelley Fu.

Notes on
The Story of the White Snake

The Chinese used to believe that if one's spirit is trained long enough, one can achieve godhood. Not only can a god live forever without aging, he or she also has magic powers and can transform into any form, man or beast, and ride clouds to all corners of the world. Gods can also control the weather. However, training to be a god requires a very long time and strict discipline. Those in training, whether human or not, must leave the human realm far behind and live a very simple life. Thus, one can have a heart full of peace and train energetically.

After hundreds or thousands of years, one can achieve a very high level of training and finally attain godhood. During training, one must not be disturbed or subject to temptation. If training is interrupted, godhood can never be achieved. That is why in the beginning of the story, Bai Su-Tzin and Shao Chin live on O Mei Mountain. The peaceful and ascetic conditions on this mountain make it a perfect place to train the spirit for godhood.

The Chinese regarded snakes in much the same way as dragons—they could be either good or bad. These nonhuman creatures are traditionally seen as monsters but not necessarily evil ones. They could redeem themselves through virtuous deeds or thoughts and thus rid themselves of their animal appearances and even become deities, such as the Dragon King of the Eastern Sea in "Journey to the West." The two snakes in this tale, Bai Su-Tzin and Shao Chin, are good snakes. They have been humanized by their training and are kinder than most people. Although the two snakes are on the way to achieving divinity, they sacrifice immortality in order to live in the human realm. The ultimate downfall of the two snakes through the intervention of Fa Hai can be interpreted in several ways.

Because Fa Hai is a Buddhist monk, his resentment of the two snakes may represent the clash between Buddhism and Taoism in China. Taoism is named after Lao Tze (603 to 531 BC), whose philosophical writings stress simplicity and naturalness as well as the relationship of man and nature.

The founder of Taoism as a religion was Zhang Dao Ling (AD first to second century), and he devoted his energies to studying gods, magic, alchemy, and the elixir of longevity. Although Lao Tze did not concern himself with these fields of study, Zhang Dao Ling applied his beliefs to the writings of Lao Tze and used the term "Taoism" for this new religion. Taoism was very popular in China thanks to Zhang Dao Ling's teachings, which appealed to the superstitious masses.

The ascetic lifestyle of the two snakes on O Mei Mountain represents a Taoist way of life. As monsters under the jurisdiction of the Celestial Ruler, they are also part of the Taoist hierarchy created by Zhang Dao Ling. Because the Celestial Ruler knows that they are good monsters, he grants the Spirit of the West permission to give the elixir of immortality to Bai Su-Tzin.

The ostensible hero of the story is Shu Shen, whose name is a pun on the words "Perhaps an Immortal." However, he is a weak character who seems unworthy of Bai Su-Tzin's great love for him. His weakness can be interpreted as representing the vacillation of the Chinese between Taoism and the Buddhism symbolized by Fa Hai.

Buddhists believe that desire is the root of all evil. When one can rid oneself of desire, one can see clearly and use this knowledge of the truth to seek the path to enlightenment. Shu Shen deliberately blinds himself to the fact that his wife and maid are snake spirits because he desires Bai Su-Tzin. When Fa Hai insists on showing Shu Shen the truth, the trouble begins. After Shu Shen loses Bai Su-Tzin, all the joy in his life also disappears. Thus, another theme emerges: it is sometimes better not to know the truth but to merely accept happiness or beauty as it comes without overanalyzing it, a very Taoist notion.

On another level, the conflict between Fa Hai and Bai Su-Tzin may represent a clash between the tenets of Buddhism and Confucian beliefs. Bai Su-Tzin wants only one thing—to be human. She wants to enjoy marital bliss and motherhood, even at the cost of immortality. Bai Su-Tzin's wish is a Confucian way of thinking, which stresses the family as one of the most basic and important elements of society. However, Fa Hai cannot stomach her masquerade in the human realm because he believes in the Buddhist notion of seeing things for what they really are.

Perhaps Fa Hai is also simply jealous of Bai Su-Tzin, whose powers are superior to his own. In fact, Fa Hai is reduced to stealing from Buddha in order to defeat the snakes. This action makes Fa Hai seem petty and unworthy as a Buddhist monk. Finally, maybe Fa Hai really does have the best interests of Shu Shen in mind. There are many Chinese stories involving animal spirits in human form that devour or ruin the men and women they come in contact with.

Shu Shen's occupation as a pharmacist is of interest because before the Sung Dynasty, most literary heroes were of noble birth. After the beginning of the Sung Dynasty (when "The Story of the White Snake" was written), teahouses flourished in China. Teahouse owners often hired storytellers to bring in business, especially merchants. To appeal to this burgeoning middle class, heroes were increasingly portrayed as common people instead of the nobility.

This story was first told during the Sung Dynasty and retold by Feng Meng Lung (AD 1574 to 1646). Similar to Wu Cheng En, who wrote the "Journey to the West," Feng Meng Lung was looked down upon by most scholars of the Ming Dynasty (AD 1368 to 1644) for writing in *bai hua* rather than *wen yen wen*. Nowadays, his version of this story is the most elaborate and famous.

The Heavenly River

牛郎織女

On a clear summer night, the Milky Way shines in the sky like a heavenly river. In fact, the Chinese call the Milky Way *Tien Ho*, or the Heavenly River. They also called it *Yin Ho*, or the Silver River. The story of its creation involves a poor cowherd.

This cowherd once lived happily in a small farming village with his older brother on an inheritance. However, his life of contentment soon changed. The older brother fell in love with a local maid who was very greedy, but she hid her rapaciousness behind a façade of demure sweetness. The older brother and this maid were soon married. In no time, he was quite under his wife's thumb.

The wife's greed soon manifested itself. She longed to get rid of the younger brother so that she and her husband could share the inheritance alone. She constantly scolded him and made her husband side with her against him. But the young man still loved his older brother and would not leave. Besides, where else could he go? The stocky, vulgar peasant maids in his village did not appeal to him, and he refused to marry.

One day, the older brother's wife went into town and bought a packet of poison from the pharmacy. That night, she put the poison into the younger brother's rice bowl. He knew of her thinly veiled dislike for him and her greed, and he did not trust her. Every day, he fed a bit of rice from his dinner to the family dog before eating it himself. On that night, the dog immediately fell ill after eating the rice. It crawled outside in agony, where it died on the family's doorstep. Needless to say, the younger brother went hungry.

When the wife saw that her scheme had failed, she was very unhappy and began to torment the younger brother day and night. She started treating him like a servant and never let him have any money. Soon, his clothes became very ragged, and he was always hungry. He was sent out every day to tend the family's old yellow cow. Gradually, he began to be very fond of the creature and even slept in the stable at night with his head resting against her side.

To make a little money, he offered to tend the cows of other families too. In time, the entire village began calling him the cowherd. With his shabby clothes and leading a motley assortment of cattle, he really did seem like a cowherd.

When the wife found out that her brother-in-law was making money, she demanded that he share it with her and her husband.

"But it's only a little bit! I need that money to buy food for myself. I'm always starving!" he protested.

The wife lost her temper. "You selfish ingrate! We let you live with us and you deny us a share of your earnings," she yelled. The cowherd was too proud to point out that she was cutting him off from his rightful share of the inheritance, but he was adamant about not handing over his hard-earned wages. There was nothing the wife could do, and she was furious. She began planning her revenge.

One day, she waited until the cowherd was gone and took the family's yellow cow into town. There, she sold her to the slaughterhouse and pocketed the money. When the cowherd found out, he rushed to the slaughterhouse. He arrived just as the cow was being led to the butcher block. The cow was shedding tears from its beautiful brown eyes. The poor cowherd couldn't bear to see the poor beast suffering. He spent all his meager savings buying back the cow.

That night when the cowherd was sleeping by the cow as usual, he dreamed that an old man came to him and said,

"You saved my life. I am a spirit disguised as your family's old yellow cow. Because I am grateful, I will give you some advice. Your life is filled with hardship, but you could marry a beautiful maid and move away from your greedy sister-in-law."

"Please tell me what I can do to bring this miracle about," begged the cowherd.

The old man resumed, "Go south until you see a clear pond. Every day, seven heavenly fairies bathe in this pond at dawn. They leave their clothes in bundles on the shore. Hide yourself until they enter the water, and grab one of the bundles. Then make your presence known. The fairy whose clothes you have will beg you to return them to her. Don't do it until she agrees to marry you."

The cowherd woke up. "What a vivid dream. It seemed so realistic!" He looked at the cow. "Did you make me have that dream?" he asked. The cow nodded. The cowherd could not believe his eyes. "Really?" he asked. The cow nodded again.

Thoughtfully, the cowherd said, "I will take your advice. After all, I have nothing to lose."

Upon hearing this, the cow licked his hand affectionately and then disappeared in a cloud of smoke. The cowherd shook his head in disbelief. "I'll miss you, yellow cow," he said sadly.

After packing a light meal, the cowherd started walking south. As twilight approached, he saw a clear pond in a beautiful garden. "This must be the place. I'll just sleep behind this tree until dawn," he thought as he settled himself for the night.

At dawn, he was awakened by the sound of splashing and maidenly laughter. Amazed, he looked out from behind his hiding place to see seven lovely women bathing and playing in the pond. They were so beautiful that the cowherd's breath failed him. As the old yellow cow had predicted, seven colorful bundles of clothing were neatly stacked in front of his tree. Quickly he ran out from behind the tree and grabbed one.

All the fairies screamed. Each one quickly grabbed her clothes and then disappeared—except for one. She groped for her bundle in panic until she saw that it was in the cowherd's hands.

"Please sir, give me back my clothes. I cannot leave without them!" she wailed. She blushed until she looked like a pink pearl glowing in the water. Her loveliness quite dazzled the cowherd. He shook his head to clear it.

Remembering the cow's advice, he firmly said, "I'm sorry, I can't do that."

"I'll make you rich if you give them back," she pleaded. "Is it power you want? I can have you appointed as a powerful government official!" She went on to offer him everything she could think of, even immortality, but the cowherd just kept on shaking his head.

The maiden thought to herself, "This cowherd is no ordinary man. He must have help from the gods or he wouldn't have known how to trap me. He is really quite handsome despite his poverty-stricken appearance."

Finally, she modestly lowered her head and said, "Sir, if you give me back my clothes, I will marry you."

The cowherd was overjoyed. "I promise to make you a good husband," he said happily.

The fairy maiden was actually the daughter of the Celestial Ruler. She was also the Goddess of Weaving. The Celestial Ruler himself married them. He gave them a beautiful house in the Celestial Realm, and they received many magical and wonderful wedding gifts, guaranteeing them a life of ease. The Celestial Ruler also graciously appointed the cowherd as the God of Cowherds, a post as important as his wife's.

"Take your duties seriously. If you do not fulfill your obligations, your actions will have dire consequences for the human realm," he solemnly warned the young couple.

"We promise to do our best," they joyfully replied. And they began their new life together.

At first, the weaving maid and the cowherd tried to obey the Celestial Ruler and dutifully spent each day overseeing their responsibilities. The cowherd kept a watchful eye on the activities of all the earthly cowherds, and the weaving maid did the same with the looms of earthly maidens. However, they were so much in love that each moment they spent apart was torture. When they were finally allowed to be together, they could barely tear themselves apart from each other.

One day, they decided to cut their daily duties down by one hour so that they could spend one hour more together. Soon, they each spent less and less time at their appointed activities. It was not long before they agreed not to show up at work at all and instead to spend the entire day together. Predictably enough, they soon abandoned their posts entirely and frolicked all day and all night together without giving a thought to the consequences.

On earth, chaos struck. Cowherds began losing their animals, which wandered off or fell ill, and weaving maidens had huge tangles in their looms, making the production of cloth impossible. People suffered because they could get no meat or milk from their lost livestock, and their clothes became very shabby indeed when cloth became scarce. In desperation, they sent up piteous prayers to the Celestial Ruler.

When the Celestial Ruler heard their pleas, he was furious. He commanded the cowherd and the weaving maid to appear before him in his imposing palace.

"You have shirked your duties! I warned you that your actions would have dire effects. People everywhere are suffering because of your selfish laziness!" he roared at them.

Frightened and ashamed, they hung their heads and turned red. The weaving maid pleaded, "Please Father, do not punish my husband too severely. It is my fault. I love him too much and –"

"No!" the cowherd interrupted. "It's my fault entirely. You see, I am the one who persuaded my wife to spend the day at home instead of—"

"Silence!!" bellowed the Celestial Ruler. "Can't you see that you are only enraging me more with your pathetic excuses?! Your love has blinded you to the needs of others, and you think only of yourselves. You must be punished for your thoughtlessness. I decree that you shall see each other only one night a year, and that night shall be the shortest night of the year, the Summer Solstice, which is on the seventh day of the seventh month."

He waved his hand, and husband and wife were simultaneously transported into the starry blackness of the night sky. Then a thread of water appeared between the couple. At first it was only a trickle, but it soon grew until it was a rushing torrent. The terrified couple each scrambled back from it and away from each other and had to keep scrambling as the river grew wider and wider. Soon, the river was so wide that it was fathoms deep and impossible to see the other bank. When the river stopped growing, they couldn't see each other or hear each other calling.

Heartbroken, they sadly turned away from the river and went back to their duties, which thereafter they fulfilled admirably. However, on the seventh day of the seventh month, they each hurried to the *Tien Ho*, or Heavenly River as it was now called. The cowherd had changed into his best clothes and looked handsome indeed. The weaving maid had on a beautiful new robe of iridescent rainbow-colored silk that she had spent all year weaving.

At first, each stood dismayed on opposite banks of the river, not knowing how they were supposed to cross. All of a sudden, a great flock of magpies flew down and made a living bridge out of their bodies. Tentatively, the weaving maid set one dainty foot on the bridge to see if it would hold. When it did, she let out a cry of joy and hurried across. She met her beloved husband in the middle.

That is why the Chinese say that magpies have a bald spot in late summer—their heads have been rubbed bald from being trod upon by the feet of the two eager lovers.

After their night of love, the cowherd and weaving maid sadly said goodbye to each other and returned to their posts, he on one side of the river and she on the other. And so it has gone on each year for longer than anyone can remember. The lovers fondly think about each other all year long and look forward to their next meeting. Then on the night of the Summer Solstice, they joyfully hurry across the magpie bridge to store up more happy memories for the long year ahead.

両情若是久長時
又豈在朝朝暮暮

"If the love between the two lasts forever,
Why should they mind sharing only one night each year?"
—Chin Guan (AD eleventh century), from *The Seventh Day of the Seventh Month*. Translated by Shelley Fu.

Notes on
The Heavenly River

Many Chinese love stories end sadly. Romantic love was rare in Chinese society, where marriages were mostly arranged. Thus, the cowherd and the weaving maid in this story are punished for their love for each other, which breaks the rules of the Celestial Realm and therefore creates havoc. The high regard of the Chinese for discipline and order are evident in the theme of this story, as is the subordination of individual desires to the good of society.

According to ancient Chinese astrologers, the two lovers have their own stars in the sky separated by the Milky Way. The cowherd became a star in the Aquila constellation west of the Milky Way, and the weaving maid became the star Vega east of the Milky Way.

This story gave rise to an ancient Chinese custom practiced on the seventh day of the seventh lunar month, the very day that the lovers are supposed to meet for their yearly tryst. On this day, Chinese maidens would each place a spider in a box. The next morning, the maidens would check on the spiders. If the spider wove a web in the box, it meant that the maiden had much talent at the loom and was therefore favorably regard by the Goddess of Weaving. Maidens whose boxes contained the thickest and most intricate webs were regarded as the goddess's favorites.

"The Heavenly River" explains the origin of the Milky Way and why magpies are bald. It is one of the most common and well-known Chinese stories and is told in many different versions even to this day. The earliest known rendition is by the anonymous author of the *Nineteen Poems in the Ancient Style* from the Han Dynasty (206 BC to AD 220). Tzung Lin of the sixth century wrote a more detailed account of this story in the *Almanac of Zin and Chu.*

Pronunciation Guide

I have tried to use a system of English spelling for Chinese words that closely reflects the Mandarin Chinese pronunciation. Nevertheless, readers may find the guidance below helpful.

Letter(s)	Pronunciation	Explanation
a	ä	As in "far" (for **Fa** Hai)
ai	ī	As in "hide" (for Fa **Hai**)
ao	ow	As in "how" (for **Shao** Chin)
au	ow	As in "how" (for **Yau**)
e	ə	As in "send" (for Shu **Shen**)
ei	ā	As in "say" (for O **Mei** Mountain)
hs	sh	As in "sure" (for **Hsuan** Zhang)
i	ē	As in "see" (for Ho **Yi**, Kuan **Yin**, and Shao **Chin**)
o	ô	As in "moral" (for Nu **Wo**, O Mei Mountain, and Tsang **O**)
ts	ts	As in "tse tse fly" (for **Tsang** O)
tz	tz	No exact English equivalent
u	ü	No exact English equivalent (for **Nu** Wo)
	ōō	As in "boot" (for Pan **Gu**, **Kun Lun**, and **Wu** Gan)

There are many different dialects of Chinese (such as Cantonese and Fukienese), but Mandarin Chinese is the official language of the People's Republic of China and of Taiwan, the Republic of China. In each dialect, words are pronounced differently, but all Chinese characters are written the same way, regardless of the dialect.

The *pin yin* system, which is the most popular system used to transliterate Chinese words into English today, is not used here because most Westerners find letters used in the *pin yin* system, such as "x," "q," and "c," pronounced quite differently under this system than they are usually pronounced in English.

List of Characters

Bai Su-Tzin (By Soo-Tzin): A white [*bai*] snake spirit in disguise as a beautiful woman; wife of Shu Shen (The Story of the White Snake)

Buddha, God of Boundless Light: The god and founder of Buddhism; an omnipotent Being (Journey to the West; The Story of the White Snake)

Celestial Ruler: Ruler of the Celestial Realm; father of the nine suns and the weaving maid; created the Milky Way and smoothed the sea bottom; second only to Buddha in power (Ho Yi the Archer; Journey to the West; The Story of the White Snake; The Heavenly River)

Cowherd: A poor mortal who later became the husband of the weaving maid and son-in-law of the Celestial Ruler; appointed by the Celestial Ruler as the God of Cowherds (The Heavenly River)

Dragon King of the Eastern Sea: Immortal dragon who rules the Eastern Sea from an underwater jade palace; famous for his generosity; son of the Dragon Mother (Journey to the West)

Dragon Mother: Mother of the Dragon King of the Eastern Sea (Journey to the West)

Fa Hai (Fa Hi): Abbot of the Gold Mountain Monastery; a legendary Buddhist monk with supernatural powers (The Story of the White Snake)

Feng Men (Foong Moong): A mortal who became Ho Yi's archery student (Ho Yi the Archer)

Fu Fei (Fu Fay): Goddess of the Lo River; wife of Old Man River (Ho Yi the Archer)

God of Fire: Enemy of the God of Water, whom he defeated in battle, thus causing the God of Water to knock down one of the pillars that hold up the sky (Nu Wo, the Mother of Mankind)

God of Merit: Hsuan Zhang, who Buddha assigned to this post as a reward (Journey to the West)

God of Water: Enemy of the God of Fire; butted his head against one of the pillars that hold up the sky, thus causing the sky to fall (Nu Wo, the Mother of Mankind)

God Victorious in Conflict: Shun Wu Koong, who Buddha assigned to this post as a reward (Journey to the West)

Great Sage Equal to Heaven: Shun Wu Koong, who was given this title by the Celestial Ruler (Journey to the West)

Ho Yi (Ho Yee): God of Archery who later became mortal; the greatest archer in Chinese mythology; husband of Tsang-O; teacher of Feng Men; favorite of Yau (Ho Yi the Archer)

Hsuan Zhang (Shuan Zhang): A historical figure who was a monk living during the T'ang Dynasty (AD 618 to 907); arguably the greatest translator in Chinese history for translating the Buddhist Scriptures from Sanskrit into Chinese; master of Shun Wu Koong during the trip to India to retrieve the Scriptures (Journey to the West)

King of the Dead: Comparable to Pluto in Greek mythology; executes orders of the Celestial Ruler with regard to the Register of the Dead (Journey to the West)

Kuan Yin (Guan Yeen): Goddess of Mercy and Buddha's helper (Journey to the West)

Master of the Cave of the Slanting Moon and Three Stars: Shun Wu Koong's first teacher (Journey to the West)

Monkey King: Shun Wu Koong, who ruled the monkeys of Flower and Fruit Mountain (Journey to the West)

Nu Wo (see Pronunciation Guide): A goddess who created mankind and mended the sky after it collapsed (Nu Wo, the Mother of Mankind)

Old Man River: God of all the rivers in the world; husband of Fu Fei (Ho Yi the Archer)

Pan Gu (Pahn Goo): Creator of the world who imposed order on Chaos; ancestor of all living beings (Pan Gu and the Creation)

Queen of Heaven: Wife of the Celestial Ruler; mother of the nine suns; has birthday party ruined by Shun Wu Koong (Ho Yi the Archer; Journey to the West)

Shao Chin (Shao Cheen): A green [*chin*] snake spirit in disguise as a pretty maid; maid of Bai Su-Tzin and Shu Shen (The Story of the White Snake)

Shu Shen (see Pronunciation Guide): A mortal who became the husband of Bai Su-Tzin and the master of Shao Chin; his name literally means "Perhaps an Immortal" (The Story of the White Snake)

Shun Wu Koong (Suen Woo Koong): Stone monkey who became the Monkey King; studied with the Master of the Cave of the Slanting Moon and Three Stars; later became disciple of Buddha and Hsuan Zhang's bodyguard; appointed by Buddha as the God Victorious in Conflict (Journey to the West)

Spirit of the West: Strange being with long, messy hair, tiger's teeth, and a tail; lives in cave on Kun Lun Mountain; makes elixir of immortality; sometimes disguises itself as a friendly old woman (Ho Yi the Archer; The Story of the White Snake)

Tsang-O (see Pronunciation Guide): A goddess who became mortal as the wife of Ho Yi; later becomes goddess stranded on the moon; eventually referred to by the Chinese as the Goddess of the Moon (Ho Yi the Archer; The Man in the Moon)

Weaving Maid: Fairy daughter of the Celestial Ruler; Goddess of Weaving; wife of the cowherd (The Heavenly River)

Wu Gan (Woo Gahn): Boy who was mortal and then became the Man in the Moon (The Man in the Moon)

Yau (Yow): A historical figure who was one of the greatest statesmen and rulers during China's Golden Age; supposedly ruled for 100 years (2357 to 2257 BC) (Ho Yi the Archer)

Yellow cow: Spirit disguised as a yellow cow to help the cowherd (The Heavenly River)

Further Reading and Multimedia Resources Guide

Young Readers

Alexander, Lloyd. *The Remarkable Journey of Prince Jen.* New York: Dutton Children's Books, 1991.

Carpenter, Frances. *Tales of a Chinese Grandmother.* Boston, MA: Charles E. Tuttle, 1972.

Goldstein, Peggy. *Long Is a Dragon: Chinese Writing for Children.* Berkeley, CA: Pacific View Press, 1992.

He, Liyi. *The Spring of Butterflies and Other Folktales of China's Minority Peoples.* Edited by Neil Philip. New York: Lothrop, Lee and Shepard, 1987.

Jianing, Chen, and Yang Yang Jianing. *The World of Chinese Myths.* Chinese-English edition. Beijing, China: Beijing Language and Culture University Press, 1995.

Long, Hua. *The Moon Maiden and Other Asian Folktales.* San Francisco, CA.: China Books, 1993.

Major, John S. *The Land and People of China.* New York: HarperCollins Children's Books, 1989.

McCunn, Ruthanne Lum. *Chinese Proverbs.* Illustrated by You-Shan Tang. San Francisco, CA: Chronicle Books, 1992.

Ramos, Lindsey. *Four Chinese Children's Stories.* Santa Cruz, CA: Little People's Press, 1991.

Stepanchuk, Carol. *Red Eggs and Dragon Boats: Celebrating Chinese Festivals.* Berkeley, CA: Pacific View Books, 1993.

Tan, Amy. *The Moon Lady.* Illustrated by Gretchen Shields. New York: Macmillan Publishing Company, 1992.

Waterlow, Julia. *China.* Danbury, CT: Franklin Watts Inc., 1990.

Xuan, Yong-Shen. *The Dragon Cover and Other Chinese Proverbs.* Chinese–English edition. Auburn, CA: Shen's Books, 1999.

Yee, Paul. *Tales from the Gold Mountain: Stories of the Chinese in the New World.* Illustrated by Simon Ng. New York: Macmillan Publishing Company, 1990.

Yep, Laurence. *American Dragons: Twenty-Five Asian American Voices.* New York: HarperCollins Children's Books, 1993.

Yep, Laurence. *The Junior Thunder Lord.* Illustrated by Robert Van Nutt. Mahwah, NJ: BridgeWater, 1994.

Yep, Laurence. *The Man Who Tricked a Ghost.* Illustrated by Isadore Seltzer. Mahwah, NJ: BridgeWater, 1994.

Yep, Laurence. *The Rainbow People.* Illustrated by David Wiesner. New York: Harper & Row, 1989.

Yep, Laurence. *Tiger Woman.* Illustrated by Robert Roth. Mahwah, NJ: BridgeWater, 1995.

Older Readers

Birch, Cyril. *Anthology of Chinese Literature.* Two volumes. New York: Grove Press Inc., 1972.

Chan, Jeffery P., ed. *The Big Aiiieeee!: An Anthology of Asian American Literature.* San Mateo, CA: JACP, Inc., 1992.

Chang, H.C., comp. *Chinese Literature.* Three volumes. New York: Columbia University Press, 1977.

Ch'eng-En, Wu. *Monkey.* Translated by Arthur Waley. New York: Grove Press Inc., 1958.

Eberhard, Wolfram. *Folktales of China.* Chicago, IL: University of Chicago Press, 1973.

Giskin, Howard. *Chinese Folktales*. Lincolnwood, IL: NTC Publishing Group, 1997.

Gordon, Ruth. *Time Is the Longest Distance: An Anthology of Poems*. New York: Charlotte Zolotow/HarperCollins, 1991.

Kingston, Maxine Hong. *Trip Master Monkey, His Fake Book*. New York: Alfred A. Knopf, 1989.

Lindsay, William, and Guo Baofu. *The Terracotta Army of the First Emperor of China*. Odyssey Publications, 1999.

Mair, Victor H., ed. *The Columbia Anthology of Chinese Literature*. New York: Columbia University Press, 1994.

Teacher's Resources

Angell, Carole S. *Celebrating Around the World: A Multicultural Handbook*. Golden, CO: Fulcrum Publishing, Inc., 1996.

Chow, Claire. Leaving Deep Water: *The Lives of Asian American Women at the Crossroads of Two Cultures*. New York: Dutton Books, 1998.

Dresser, Norrine. *Multicultural Celebrations*. New York: Three Rivers Press, 1999.

Eberhard, Wolfram. *Dictionary of Chinese Symbols*. New York: Routledge, Kegan & Paul, 1988.

Five College Center for East Asian Studies. *East Asia in New England*. Northampton, MA: Newsletter of the Five College Center for East Asian Studies.

Gaskins, Pearl Fuyo, ed. *What Are You?—Voices of Mixed Race Young People*. New York: Henry Holt and Co., 1999.

Hong, Maria. *Growing Up Asian American: An Anthology*. New York: Avon Books, 1995.

Liu, Eric. *The Accidental Asian: Notes of a Native Speaker*. New York: Random House, 1998.

Pan, Lynn. *The Encyclopedia of the Chinese Overseas.* Cambridge, MA: Harvard University Press, 1999.

Wei, William. *The Asian American Movement.* Philadelphia, PA: Temple University Press, 1994.

Multimedia Resources

Children's Songs: China. Two sound CDs of 22 Chinese songs. China Records Corporation, 1996.

China—A Century of Change. Three videos, 120 minutes each. PBS Video Series Documentary. 1997.

Multicultural Peoples of North America. 15-volume video series, 30 minutes each. 1993.

Sing-Learn Chinese. By Trio Jan Jeng and Selina Yoon. 22 familiar songs. Master Communications, 1997.

Touring China. Video. 68 minutes. Questar, 1998.

Selected Websites

Asian Studies Virtual Library
http://www.ciolek.com/SearchEngines.html

Reference Guide to China and Related Websites
http://ChinaSite.com

Mythology Website
http://www.windows.umich.edu/cgi-in/tour_def/mythology/china.html.

Chinese Culture Website
http://chineseculture.tqn.com/msu682.htm

Chinese Education and Research Network Site
http://www.edu.cn

Bejing University Site
http://www.pku.edu.cn

San Diego Chinese Museum Site
http://www.sandiego-online.com

Source Notes

As discussed earlier, the stories in this book were derived from many sources, including my memory and imagination. However, the sources below were a great help and deserve to be cited.

Anonymous. *Nu Wo Mends the Sky*. Chinese edition. Hong Kong: Seagull Publishing Company, n.d.

Chang, Richard F. *Chinese Mythical Stories*. Chinese edition. Urbana, IL: University of Illinois Press, 1980.

Ch'eng–En, Wu. *Monkey*. Translated by Arthur Waley. New York: Grove Press Inc., 1958.

Fei, Xu. *Lady White*. Translated by Xu Guo-Hua. Chinese–English edition. Hong Kong: Hai Feng Publishing Company, 1985.